Ishtar's Odyssey

by Arnold Ytreeide

for Advent

Jotham's Journey

Bartholomew's Passage

Tabitha's Travels

Ishtar's Odyssey

for Easter

Amon's Adventure

Ishtar's Odyssey

A Family Story for Advent

Arnold Ytreeide

Ishtar's Odyssey: A Family Story for Advent

Cover design: Hile Illustration and Design, Ann Arbor, MI
Interior illustrations: Ryan Hill

Published by Kregel Publications, a division of Kregel Inc., 2450 Oak Industrial Dr. NE, Grand Rapids, MI 49505.

Within the story narrative, Scripture quotations are from either the King James Version or the *New International Version* cited above.

Other than biblical characters and events, the persons and events portrayed in this work are the creations of the author, and any resemblance to persons living or dead is purely coincidental.

Library of Congress Cataloging-in-Publication Data
Ytreeide, Arnold.
Ishtar's odyssey : a story for Advent / by Arnold Ytreeide.
pages cm
1. Magi—Juvenile literature. 2. Advent—Prayers and devotions—Juvenile literature. 3. Families—Prayers and devotions—Juvenile literature. I. Title.
BT315.2.Y77 2015 242.332—dc23 2015008779

ISBN 978-0-8254-4393-0

Printed in the United States of America
5 6 7 / 25 24 23 22 21

For Shayla.
For Gemma.
For Silje.
For Elaena.
For all my grandchildren
not yet born.
And for all children everywhere.

Before the Story

Stir us up, O Lord, to make ready for your only begotten Son. May we be able to serve you with purity of soul through the coming of him who lives and reigns.

Advent Prayer

Advent. *Adventus. Ecce advenit Dominator Dominus.* Behold, the Lord the Ruler is come. Reaching back two millennia to the birth of the Christ child, and forward to his reign on earth, the tradition of Advent is a three-fold celebration of the birth of Jesus, his eventual second coming to earth, and of his continued presence in our lives here and now. God in our past, God in our future, God in our present.

Advent.

It started with people going hungry to purify themselves and prepare themselves for holy living. A *fast*, we call it, and such a fast was ordered by the Council of Saragossa in A.D. 381. For three weeks before Epiphany (a feast in January celebrating the divine revelation of Jesus to the gentile Magi) the people were to fast and pray in preparation. The tradition spread to all of France in 581 by decree of the Council of Macon, and to Rome and beyond thereafter. Gregory the First refined the season to its present form in about 600 when he declared that it should start the fourth Sunday before Christmas.

Fasting is no longer a part of Advent in most homes and churches (though it wouldn't be a bad idea). For us, Advent means taking a few minutes each day, for the three or four weeks before Christmas, to center our thoughts on Truth Incarnate lying in a feeding trough in Bethlehem. It's a time of worship, a time of reflection, a time of focus, and a time of family communion. In the midst of December's commotion and stress, it's a few moments to stop, catch your breath, and renew your strength from the only One who can provide true strength.

Ishtar's Odyssey is one tool you can use to implement a time of Advent in your family—whether yours is a traditional family structure or one of the many combinations of fathers and mothers, stepparents and grandparents, and guardians and children that make up today's families. You can use this story during Advent even if your family is just you.

Set aside a few minutes each day, beginning the fourth Sunday before Christmas (see the chart on page 176) to light the Advent candles, read the Ishtar story and devotional for that day, and pray together. You can also use an Advent calendar (see "Advent Customs," page 15), sing a favorite Christ-centered carol (Frosty's a nice guy, but has no place in Advent), and have a time of family sharing.

Our family set aside fifteen minutes each night before the youngest child went to bed. Our Advent wreath had a traditional place on a table next to the living room reading chair. The children took turns each night lighting the candles and reading the calendar, adding that day's window at the end. By the light of the Advent candles I read the last few lines of the previous day's Ishtar story, then the story and devotion for that day. Afterward Mom led in prayer as we all held hands. We closed by singing one verse of a carol. The youngest child then lit her own "bedside" candle from the Advent candles and made her way to bed by candlelight (being old enough to know how to use a candle safely). Even when work or visiting took us out of town, we carried the book and a candle with us and kept our Advent tradition. Sometimes we even shared our tradition with those we were visiting.

Simple, short, spiritual. A wonderful way to keep the shopping and traffic and rehearsals and concerts and parties and preparations of December in balance with the reality of God in our lives—past, present, and future.

Advent. *Adventus. Ecce advenit Dominator Dominus.* Behold, the Lord the Ruler is come. May God richly bless you and your family as you prepare to celebrate the birth of Christ!

About the Magi

> During the time of King Herod, Magi from the east came to Jerusalem and asked, “Where is the one who has been born king of the Jews? We saw his star when it rose and have come to worship him.”
>
> Matthew 2:1–2

Who were these Magi? Where did they come from? Why did they come to worship a foreign king? Were there three or seven or twelve magi? When exactly did they arrive? These are questions to which we’ll never know the answers until we get to heaven.

Because of that, *Ishtar’s Odyssey* has very little fact, and a lot of fiction, when it comes to the magi themselves. We just don’t know. I’ve chosen to keep the western tradition of three magi, and I’ve chosen to make them from Persia, specifically the Parthian dynasty of Persia. In that sense, the story is fairly historically accurate—the foods, architecture, warriors, politics, social mores, and caravans of the era are depicted accurately with only a bit of literary license.

But details about the magi described in Scripture? We simply don’t have any.

The question is, does it really matter? From a spiritual sense, does it matter if there were three or twelve? Does it matter if they arrived the night of Jesus’ birth or a few months after?

I think what this story tells us is that God provided ways for *all* people to come to Jesus. His birth—and the *celebration* of his birth—is not for any one people or for any one church. He came to earth for all people, and accepts all people wherever they are in their own spiritual journey.

He can draw people to himself no matter where they live.

So it might be important to let your children know that the events and most of the people of *Ishtar's Odyssey* are fictitious. But it's equally important to let them know that the miracles God worked in lives, and still works in lives today, are very real.

Making Connections

At JothamsJourney.com you'll find maps, photos, and other documents to help your family connect to the story more directly.

But there's another way you might try to make the story come alive for your children.

Ishtar's Odyssey is largely a journey of food. Cuisine. Eating.

Ishtar has been raised in a palace far removed from the common culture, and rich in the finest foods. He's used to having his choice of exotic dishes available on command, and thinks nothing of asking for that which takes a great deal of effort—and money—to prepare.

Until his trek begins.

When Ishtar suddenly finds himself on a smelly, dirty caravan crossing an endless desert, there are no more fine foods or sweet desserts. There is only millet—a bland grain cooked into a thin porridge.

I thought it might be fun—and meaningful—for your children to experience *Ishtar's Odyssey* the way Ishtar largely does: through food. The chart below suggests foods you might use to help enhance the story during some days' readings. Depending on the ages and courage of your children as well as the time and money you want to commit, you might prepare the actual dish, searching the internet for a recipe you like, or you might prepare a similar but more kid-friendly food to simulate the food described in the story.

Use these ideas as meals, accompaniment to meals, a snack before the reading, or a food tasting as part of your Advent devotional time. You could even stop in the middle of the story when a food is described and give it a taste. To be most authentic, spread a blanket or tablecloth on the floor, surround it with pillows and couch cushions, and recline around your meal—utensils optional—with a fingerbowl of warm water for each person.

While experimenting with something new is great for kids, the goal is for this to be a positive and memorable experience for them. The point is to show the important role food played in Ishtar's life, and how he learned from it. If forcing your child to gag down *haleem* will cause him or her to hate Advent, using the more familiar, kid-friendly options might be the better choice.

However you do it, we'd love to hear about your experiences and experiments in the comments section at JothamsJourney.com!

PERSIAN FOOD		
DAY	**AUTHENTIC**	**SIMILAR**
Week 1, Sunday The first day of the story. Ishtar describes a banquet. Fix a dinner with as many of these as your stamina and stomach can tolerate. Great way to start Advent!	Polo (rice; many recipes)	Rice pilaf; boxed flavored rice
	Nan-e barbari (flatbread)	Naan Indian bread; pita bread
	Fresh fruit	
	Mokhalafat (accompaniments)	Sliced tomato and cucumber, pickles, olives, chopped herbs, hard-boiled eggs
	Koofteh berenji	Meatballs (especially mixed with rice)
	Mahi sefeed	Pan-fried whitefish; fish sticks or fillets
	Torshi bademjan	Stuffed eggplant; stuffed dill pickles; any pickled vegetable
	Nogha	Nougat; favorite chewy candy bar
	Chai	Spiced or herbal tea
Week One - Monday	Nan-e barbari	Naan Indian bread; pita bread
	Haleem (with lamb)	Thick lentil, pea, or bean soup; hash
	Dates, pomegranates, peaches, apricots	Any dried fruit
	Kebab	Any type of meat on a skewer with fruits or vegetables
	Falafel	Falafel; hummus
	Goat milk	Any milk
	Chai	Spiced or herbal tea

Week One - Wednesday	Zulbia	Doughboys, funnel cakes, or cinnamon elephant ears (with honey for dipping)
Week One - Thursday	Nan-e barbari	Naan Indian bread; pita bread
	Pomegranate jam	Any favorite jam
	Reshteh khoshkar	Any cookies with spices and/or nuts, such as snickerdoodles or snowballs
	Chai	Spiced or herbal tea
Week One - Saturday Week Two - Sunday	Millet porridge	Any seed or grain, such as quinoa, made into a porridge; hot instant wheat cereal
Week Two - Monday	Meat & Cheese	Beef jerky and string cheese; summer sausage and cheese curds
Week Two - Tuesday	Millet porridge	Any seed or grain, such as quinoa, made into a porridge; hot instant wheat cereal
	Roasted locusts	Gummy bugs; unsalted popcorn
	Pomegranate & pomegranate juice	Favorite fruit & juice
Week Two - Wednesday	9 triangles of Nan-e barbari	9 triangles of Naan Indian bread, pita bread, or toast
	3 small pieces grilled meat	
Week Two - Thursday	Baklava	Any pastry made with philo dough; toaster pastry; cupcake
	Gaz	Nougat; favorite chewy candy bar
Week Two - Saturday	Baklava	Any pastry made with philo dough; toaster pastry; cupcake

Week Three - Sunday	Grapes	
	Khorakeh Goosht	Beef pot roast with vegetables or beef stew
	Almonds	Any nuts
	Peaches	
Week Three - Monday	Musht ("St. Peter's Fish")	Roasted or pan-fried tilapia; fish sticks or fillets
	Laks (Lox)	Smoked salmon or any smoked fish; tuna
Week Three - Wednesday	Meat & Cheese	Beef jerky and string cheese; summer sausage and cheese curds
Week Three - Friday	Coconut	
	Dates	Raisins
Week Three - Saturday	Baklava	Any pastry made with philo dough; toaster pastry; cupcake
Christmas Day	Baklava	Any favorite Christmas cookie
	Zulbia	Any favorite Christmas pastry
	Gaz	Indian Julebi; traditional family favorite sweet

Advent Customs

Advent itself is simply any time set apart for spiritual preparation. But most people associate the word *Advent* with various traditions and customs that have grown up around Christmas in many of the world's cultures. Early in history these customs took the forms of fasts and feasts. Today they most often take the forms of candles, wreaths, and calendars.

Most churches and families use Advent candles to celebrate the season. Five are used in all, one for each week of Advent and the fifth for Christmas Day. The first, second, and fourth candles are violet, symbolizing penitence. The third is pink, symbolizing joy, and the Christmas Day candle is white, symbolizing the purity of Christ.

Advent candles are usually part of an Advent wreath. While some traditions hang the wreath, it is most commonly used flat, on a table. The circle of the wreath represents the hope of eternal life we have through Christ. The circle itself is made of evergreen branches, symbolizing the abundant life Jesus promised us in the here-and-now. The first four candles are positioned along the outside ring of the wreath and the fifth is placed in the center.

Some traditions use a slanted board instead of a wreath to hold the candles. The board is about four inches by twelve, and raised six inches on one end. Four holes are drilled along the length of the board for the first four candles, and the fifth candle is placed at the top.

Another candle tradition uses one candle for each day of Advent. Any color of candle can be used, but the Sunday candles are usually of a special design and color. The candles can either be placed along a mantel, or in holes drilled in a log. Each night during devotions one more candle is lit. By Christmas Day, the candles give bright testimony to and reminder of the evenings of devotion you've spent together as a family.

Advent calendars are popular with children and teach them the Christmas story in an active way. Also called an "Advent house," the calendar is shaped like a house, with a window for each day of Advent. Behind each window is a small portion of the Christmas story (usually from the book of Luke). Each night the family reads the story from these windows, ending by opening the window for that day.

A Note to Parents: Jesus was not born in an amusement park or religious retreat. He was born into a world of sin, darkness, and death. Indeed, his own birth caused the death of many male children as Herod sought to kill the new King. So it is not the intent of *Ishtar's Odyssey* to present a heaven-like world where everyone lives in purity and harmony. While the story is fun and adventurous, and has the most happy of endings, it does take place in the real world: there is greed, there is cruelty, there is sin. The point is not to cover up the dark side of life, but rather to show how the love of God and his son Jesus Christ are the *light* of our lives.

Most children over the age of seven have been exposed to far worse violence in movies, TV, and cartoons than you'll find in this story. However, if your children are younger, or are particularly sensitive, I suggest you preview each day's reading so that you might skip or summarize the few more tragic parts. You may also want to talk with your children about the events in the story, to help them understand that sometimes bad things happen to people, but that you and God are there to love them and protect them.

In any event, it is my sincere hope and prayer that you and God together can use this story to teach your children just how much God loves them and how close he is to us, even in times of tragedy.

Especially in times of tragedy.

May God richly bless your Advent time together!

Pronunciation Guide: Foreign names can sometimes be difficult to pronounce. If you grew up in a Western culture, your mouth may not even be *capable* of pronouncing these names correctly. But for those who would like to conform to at least a pretense of a guide (admittedly inaccurate), these are some of the names you'll encounter in *Ishtar's Odyssey*:

Ishtar = ISH-tar
Salamar = SAL-uh-mar
Kazeem = kuh-ZEEM
Varta = VAHR-tuh
Jodhpur = JAWD-purr
Bozan -boe-ZAWN
Rasad = ruh-SAWD
Faraj = far-AWJ
Jotham = JAW-thum
Decha = DECK-uh
Konarak = KAHN-uh-rack
Amaranth = AM-uh-ranth
Zelzele = zell-ZEAL
Seleucia = sell-OO-see-uh
Tericheae = TARE-i-kigh

A Rich Diet

Light the first violet candle.

Ishtar sat on his golden throne, dressed in royal robes with a crown of jewels on his head. He looked across the throne room, filled from wall to wall with his subjects shouting his name in admiration. "Ishtar! Ishtar!" They sang his praises not out of force or duty, but because they loved him. King Ishtar, King of Kings, ruler of all Persia, only ten years old but already the protector, provider, and savior of all his people. Never had there been a king so . . .

"Ishtar!"

At the sharp sound of his name Ishtar flinched, which caused his head to go under and water to go up his nose. He kicked and splashed until finally his feet found the bottom of the pool. He stood coughing and sputtering, wiping the water from his eyes. That's when he saw his bodyguard, Kazeem, standing over him on the side of the pool.

"Many apologies," Kazeem said. "I did not mean to startle you, but I called your name three times before you heard me. Were you daydreaming of power and wealth?"

"Uh, no, of course not," Ishtar sputtered. "I . . . I was preparing my mind for my history lesson."

Kazeem just smiled, an odd smile that Ishtar suspected meant Kazeem suspected that Ishtar was not telling the entire truth. Kazeem was big for a Persian. So tall was the man that the long, curved sword hanging from his belt didn't come near to reaching the floor. His arms, resting on his hips, seemed to be the size of an elephant's legs.

"In any case," Kazeem said, "you are correct that it is time for your history lesson."

Ishtar didn't argue, mostly because it would have done no good. While Kazeem was technically Ishtar's servant, it wasn't the same as the slaves and masters he saw from other countries. Kazeem was more of a paid worker, who could choose to quit at any time, and there were laws against mistreating servants. Besides, Kazeem had been at his side since the day he was born, and Ishtar thought of him as a friend.

Ishtar sloshed his way out of the long, rectangular pool that filled the center of his home. He lived with his father and servants on the uppermost floor of the Palace of Amaranth, where lived Sheik Konarak and all his advisors. Ishtar's father, Salamar, was the *mogan-andarzbad*, the highest-ranking advisor, and chief of all the magi.

Surrounding the pool were sleeping chambers, study rooms, and a large banquet hall where Salamar, with Ishtar at his side, would often entertain exotic guests. Amaranth was a seaport on the Arabian coast, a city that saw many merchants and traders pass through her gates. In fact it was the "magical" and nutritious seeds of the amaranth plant—brought here by Greek traders long before—that had given the city its name. Lounging on pillows through hundreds of banquets, Ishtar had learned many facts like this, and the ways of many different cultures from both east and west.

"Quickly now," Kazeem scolded. "You must not keep Hormoz waiting."

Hormoz. An expert in history, and one of Ishtar's several tutors. While he was allowed a swim in the pool in the heat of the afternoon, the rest of his day was spent with one tutor or another. Mathematics, science, language—it never seemed to end.

"I think if I learn much more my head may overflow and all my knowledge spill onto the floor."

"You are ten years old," Kazeem said as he escorted Ishtar to the other side of the pool. "If you live to be my age, you will discover there are always new things to be learned, and they all remain neatly stored within your head."

Kazeem stood just outside the study room as Hormoz began the lesson. It always took Hormoz a minute or two before he turned over the time marker—an invention of glass that allowed sand to fall from one chamber to another, thus marking time. Ishtar had often thought that if he could just open up the time marker and enlarge the hole through which the sand flowed, his lessons would be much shorter.

"And so we begin with a recital of the royal ancestors." Hormoz started every lesson exactly this way, and Ishtar sighed.

An hour later Ishtar was leaving his history tutor and heading for his tutor of mathematics when Salamar met him near the pool. "Father!" he exclaimed, and hugged Salamar's legs.

"*Zor bekhayr*, Ishtar," Salamar said, returning the hug. Then he took his son by the shoulders and stood him up straight. "And what did you learn in history lessons today?"

Ishtar shrugged. "Nothing."

Salamar frowned. "Then I must have Hormoz severely punished for failing to teach you."

"Oh no, no Father," Ishtar said quickly. "It is just that I already knew everything he taught today!"

Salamar's face melted into a grin and Ishtar realized his father had just been joking. Which he should have known, now that he thought about it. Out loud he said, "It's just so boring, going over the same things every day."

"It is by repeating a thing that you learn it well," Salamar said. "But for now, you will not be taking your lessons in mathematics or science. Your aunt has invited you over to play with your cousins."

Ishtar's face lit up. Only the children in the line of succession were permitted to live in the palace, and Sheik Konarak had no children of his own. The total number of children living in the palace was . . . one. The only time Ishtar got to play with others was when he visited relatives. Obviously, as part of the royal household, he could not simply go outside and play with the children in the streets.

"May my cousins come to the palace instead?" Ishtar asked. Although he was often lonely, he hated leaving the palace, even to go see his cousins. As beautiful as the city was, it was still dirty, and full of strange people. "You have nothing to fear," his father had once told him. "Then why do I need a bodyguard?" Ishtar had asked. Salamar had no answer.

But now Salamar said, "The invitation was for you to come to their home, and thus you shall."

Ishtar sighed and took his lesson parchments to his sleeping chamber.

Kazeem informed the tutors of mathematics and science that they wouldn't be needed today, then called for the bearers and led Ishtar down four flights of stairs to the courtyard. The palace was built of a reddish stone, and every door and window was topped with an ornate arch. Green trees and bushes filled the courtyard, which was decorated with colorful mosaics. A fountain in the center of the courtyard gave off a cool mist in the afternoon heat.

Ishtar climbed into his *tahtirevan*, a tall box with a seat inside and poles jutting out the front and back. Four bearers immediately lifted the poles. The metal gate—taller than four men standing on each other's shoulders—was raised, and the bearers carried Ishtar in his *tahtirevan* out into the streets, with Kazeem walking behind.

Ishtar watched the city go by through his open windows. The streets were wide and paved with stone, but very stinky from all the animals that traveled it. Along the sides were sellers of anything a Persian or visitor could possibly want—roasted meats, sharp cheeses, sweet delicacies, clothes of every color and material. As they moved along the main avenue he saw games and weapons and jewelry for sale. For a price, you could even get your future told, though Ishtar's father had warned him many times that such fortunetellers were frauds.

Being a seaport directly on the trade routes, Amaranth was full of all kinds of people: Greeks, Asians, Africans, even Romans, though the Persian Empire and the Roman Empire were always on the verge of war.

The shadows hadn't moved very far by the time Ishtar reached the home of his cousins. They spent the afternoon playing King's Ransom—one of many games Salamar had brought home with him from his travels. The sun was getting low in the sky when Kazeem said it was time to return to the palace. Many of the sellers' stalls were closing, and children played in the mostly empty streets. As they passed one group of boys about Ishtar's age he heard them talking.

"There goes that fancy boy Ishtar," one boy said.

"He even has a girl's name!" another added.

Then they chanted his name in a mocking way—"Ishtar, Ishtar, Ishtar."

Back at the palace, Ishtar was silent as he put on a clean coat for dinner.

"You are quiet tonight."

Ishtar jumped at the sound of his father's voice behind him.

"Usually I can hear you babbling to Kazeem from the other side of the palace."

"I . . . I was thinking about something," Ishtar said.

"And what great thoughts so occupy the mind of my son that he has no room for talk?"

Ishtar looked away. Part of him was embarrassed to answer the question, but part of him really wanted to. Finally the second part won.

"Is . . . is my name a girl's name?"

Salamar sighed deeply, then sat on his son's bed. "Names can behave strangely," he said after a long pause. "In one country they can be one thing, in another country they can be just the opposite."

"But is *Ishtar* a girl's name?"

Salamar gave his answer much thought while Ishtar pulled the belt around his green silk jacket. "In some countries, the name Ishtar is given to a goddess of love," Salamar said finally. "In other countries, it's the name of a god of war. But long before you were born your mother and I decided our first son would be named *Ishtar*."

At the mention of his mother, a rare occurrence, Ishtar just looked at his father.

"It was your grandfather's name," Salamar said. "We gave you that name in honor of your grandfather."

Now it was Ishtar's turn to think a long thought. "Then I shall wear the name with pride," he said finally.

Salamar stood to leave. "Good. It is not wise to worry what others might think of you, except as it may affect your relationship with them. Come now. We have guests for dinner. Merchants from several lands." *So what else is new?* Ishtar thought.

The feast that night was quite ordinary: lamb, duck, whitefish, eggplant, olives, boiled eggs, several kinds of flatbread, and lots of sauces. Everyone lounged on pillows on the floor around the food, and each had a small bowl of water beside their plate, for washing their fingers between courses. There were no actors performing Greek plays as there often were, but five musicians did play quietly in the corner. Ishtar helped himself to some more *koofteh*, scooping a meatball up with his bread. As the men ate the fine foods and drank their tea, they talked. Boring talk, Ishtar thought. And it went on forever because, as happened at so many of these dinners, the guests didn't know it was impolite to stay late into the night.

Ishtar's favorite dishes were the desserts. At least three at every meal—including *nogha*, made from the sweet sap of a rare plant, mixed with ground nuts, and spread between two crisp wafers. It was chewy and nutty.

"Ishtar, no more *nogha*," his father whispered after Ishtar's third helping.

Three of the guests were Jewish merchants from Palestine. Every time someone would mention the gods, one of them would say, "Hear, O Israel, the Lord is our God, the Lord is one."

The third time the merchant said this a trader from Kashgar said, "You Jews say there is but one god, yet he has abandoned you. Would it not be wise to turn to another? Samantabhadra, perhaps. Or the Persian god Ameretat."

"The Lord is our God, the Lord is one," the Jewish merchant said again. "He has not abandoned us. He has promised us a Messiah, one who will save us some day."

"Someday soon, perhaps?"

"Oh no, the prophecy of the Messiah shall not be fulfilled for many centuries," the merchant scoffed.

Ishtar was almost glad when Kazeem finally fetched him for his astronomy lesson. He followed his bodyguard to the other side of the pool and up a spiral stairway made of stone, to the roof of the palace. Ishtar looked out across the city, lit only by starlight and a sliver of moon just peeking over the horizon, such that all the tall buildings were outlined in silver. Beyond that he saw the Akhzar Sea, its waves lapping against the shore.

Since astronomy was the study of the stars, and since stars only appear at night, astronomy lessons were almost always taught at night. Ishtar's tutor for these lessons was a rickety old man that Ishtar was sure must have been born ages *before* the stars. Alim was his name, and his lessons were always the same. He sat in a chair and read a book by lamplight while making Ishtar identify star after star.

"You're late," Alim snapped.

"We had guests for dinner," Ishtar replied, thinking as always that Alim was his servant and should treat him with more respect. But Ishtar wasn't about to tell him that.

"We must begin immediately, before the moon fully takes over the sky and there is nothing to see." With that he began giving Ishtar a string of stars to identify, not once looking up from his book.

"There are three stars above the eye of *Karzang*," Alim droned on. "They are . . . ?"

Ishtar sighed. "*Al-Waqi*, *Wasat as-Sama'*, and *Az-Zubana*."

"And above that, the two stars to the right of *Nemasp*'s ear?"

"*An-Nihal* and *Kalb ar-Rai*." Would this lesson never end?

"And the crown on the head of *Sagr* is made of three stars. What are they, please?"

Alim turned a page in his book. Ishtar stared at the sky. He knew these stars as well as his tutor—though not quite as well as his father. He knew the face of *Sagr* like he knew his own. But something was wrong . . .

"Ishtar, an answer please."

Ishtar shook his head, then picked up one of his father's seeing devices—a lens made of crystal rock in a leather tube, given to him by a man from China. The lens magnified the head of *Sagr*, but that only made Ishtar more confused.

"Ishtar! There are three stars that make up the crown of *Sagr!*"

Ishtar lowered the lens and slumped back into his chair. "No," he said, shaking his head slowly, "there are not. Tonight . . . there are *four*."

Alim set his book aside with a sigh. "Child, I had thought this a simple review, but now I see I must teach—" He had been looking at Ishtar, who was staring at the sky, but then followed Ishtar's gaze up to the constellation of *Sagr*. When his eyes landed on the fourth star now forming the crown, he stopped in mid-sentence.

Alim stared . . . and stared . . . and stared, then turned with a rush and ran back down the spiral staircase with the speed of a much younger man, yelling behind him, "Wait right there!"

Moments later Alim returned. Behind him followed Ishtar's father, his father's two brothers, and all the guests from the banquet dressed in their colorful robes. Salamar took up the looking device and aimed it where Alim pointed. Salamar gasped, then passed the device to his two brothers, who were also shocked. They began to talk quickly with one other, using words that Ishtar couldn't even understand. Finally Ishtar tugged at Salamar's trousers.

"Father! What is it? What's happening?"

Salamar looked at his son with a look Ishtar had seen only once before, the first time Ishtar had beaten him at King's Ransom, and said, "Ishtar, it seems you have discovered a star that even yesterday did not exist!"

Matthew's story of the magi who visited the baby Jesus has led to much speculation. So little is known about who they were, where exactly they came from, how many there were, or when and where they arrived, that most of what we believe about the story has been invented over the centuries. We don't even know how they "followed" the star.

But one thing we know, and the most important thing we know, is that God, in some mysterious way, led a group of Gentiles across vast spaces to bow down to Jesus, and present him with gifts.

> During the time of King Herod, Magi from the east came to Jerusalem and asked, "Where is the one who has been born king of the Jews? We saw his star in the east and have come to worship him." MATTHEW 2:1–2

Tonight we start an adventure that will take us right up to Christmas day. Like Ishtar, along the way we'll meet many people, cross a lot of ground, and learn many lessons. Ishtar has no idea what's about to happen to him, and neither do we.

But if we'll keep our hearts and minds open, listen closely for the whispers of God, and follow whatever "star" he puts before us, maybe we, too, will have some very special gifts to offer Jesus on Christmas morning.

The Star

Light the first violet candle.

Ishtar sat on his golden throne, dressed in royal robes with a crown of jewels on his head. He looked across the throne room, filled from wall to wall with his subjects, shouting his name in admiration. "Ishtar! Ishtar!" They sang his praises not out of force or duty, but . . .

"No!"

The single word, shouted by one of his uncles, woke Ishtar from his dream. He blinked several times in the bright morning sun and finally realized he was on the roof of the palace. Sometime in the night he had fallen asleep as his father, uncles, and a dozen other advisors talked their nonsensical talk about the star Ishtar had seen. Now they had charts of the night sky and many texts and scrolls spread out across several low tables, and they were still talking. Someone had covered him with a blanket. Probably Kazeem, he decided.

Ishtar stretched and sat up. His uncle Bozan was speaking quickly at Salamar in a language Ishtar did not understand. Obviously there was a disagreement.

At age ten Ishtar could already speak and understand several languages including Latin, Aramaic, Old Umbrian, Hebrew, and Greek, besides his own Persian. "Why do I have to learn Old Umbrian?" Ishtar often complained. "*No one* speaks it anymore!"

"Well then," his language tutor always replied, "you shall have an advantage when you and your enemy happen upon a road sign written only in Old Umbrian!"

Not only did Ishtar have tutors in all these tongues, but the many guests his father brought home for dinner came with their own native dialect. As a child, Ishtar had learned to talk using words from over twenty different languages before he ever realized it. He loved it when the guests would assume he couldn't understand them, and made some comment about the meal, or the city, or politics. More than once he was able to warn his father of a deceit being planned.

But the words his father and uncles spoke now were foreign even to Ishtar, except for that one word, "No!" Finally they switched back to Persian as Ishtar stood and wandered over to the group. That's when he noticed his clothes and brushed them in disgust. They were still clean, but completely wrinkled.

"It is madness to risk such a venture!" Uncle Bozan was saying. "For all we know this new king might seize the entire caravan and make slaves of us!"

Salamar slowly shook his head. "Bozan, was it you or was it I who spent seven years of his youth living amongst the Jews? Was it you or was it I who learned their ways, and their hearts?"

Ishtar's Uncle Jodhpur stepped into the conversation with a soft voice. "Bozan, Salamar is right. His knowledge and experience of this people is superior to ours. If the star were leading us to Loulan or Janjing we would surely listen to *your* counsel."

The argument continued for several more minutes until Salamar finally noticed his son. "Ah, Ishtar!" he said with a hug. "Did you dream of being a king as you slept?"

How did everyone seem to know what he was dreaming? Ishtar wondered.

Without waiting for an answer, Salamar continued. "Kazeem will take you down for the morning meal, then you must get ready. We have a busy day ahead of us."

Ishtar nodded and yawned, then followed Kazeem down the spiral stairs. They passed his sleeping chamber and Ishtar wished he could climb back into bed and dream some more. The banquet dishes had been cleared away in the dining hall, and in their place was a breakfast banquet for one—Ishtar alone. He sat at the edge of the *sofreh*—a tablecloth spread over a rug—and used a piece of flatbread to scoop up some *haleem*—a mixture of ground meat and sweetened oatmeal. As he picked at the dates and pomegranates, peaches and apricots, he planned his day. There were always lessons, of course, and he had no control over those. But between lessons, and afterward, he could do as he pleased.

Today, he decided, it would please him to play King's Ransom with Kazeem after the lesson on engineering and before the lesson in logic, then have a snack of falalfel before the lesson on politics. The lesson on politics was exceedingly boring, and required a good snack if Ishtar was to stay awake.

After his politics lesson would be lunch, of course, and Ishtar decided he'd order a kebab from the kitchen. Which is exactly what he decided every day.

Next would come his etiquette lesson, language lesson, and afternoon swim. Before dinner would be history, mathematics, science, and a game of Pasoor, played with fifty-two wooden markers, until dinner. He'd sit at the banquet for a time, then head to his astronomy lesson.

Ishtar finished planning his day about the same time he finished eating his dates and drinking his goat's milk. Of course, he had planned his day exactly the same as every other day.

"Ishtar! Stop your daydreaming!" It was Varta, the old woman in charge of meals and the household. She had an entire staff of cooks, cleaners, and servants, but when it came to Ishtar she insisted on taking care of things personally. She'd been around as long as Ishtar could remember, and almost as long as Kazeem. "Malek is waiting," she scolded. "Now get to your lessons!"

"Yes, Varta," Ishtar said, and jumped up. He would never dare talk back to or disobey her.

As he scurried around the pool to his classroom, Ishtar saw his father, uncles, and a long line of other men rushing down the spiral staircase toward the main entrance of the apartment. The men were carrying the scrolls and manuscripts he'd seen earlier, and Ishtar wanted to ask what was going on. But the look on Salamar's face told him this was not the time to interrupt. In moments they were out the door and down the grand hall, and he went to his lesson.

Two hours later Ishtar had finished his logic lesson and was in the middle of studying politics. "And so the King of Kings governs all of Persia," his tutor, Shamal, was saying, "but each region has its own king, such as our Sheik Konarak. Each king has great authority, and freedom to rule as he sees best within his region."

Ishtar rested his head on one hand while with the other he drew camels on his wax tablet. He'd never actually touched a camel—they were disgusting beasts that smelled horrible—but they were fun to draw.

Under his breath Ishtar complained, "I *know* all this . . ."

Shamal stopped for a moment, then dropped to one knee and put his face inches from Ishtar's, which drew the attention of Kazeem standing guard at the door.

"Yes, you may know all this," Shamal whispered, "but I have a secret you do not know!"

Ishtar looked up in surprise. A gust of wind blew through the many open windows of the room, scattering parchments, and for a moment Ishtar suspected his tutor had caused it.

A cool breeze was one of the benefits of living at the top of the palace, along with an absence of bad smells and very few insects. But when a *shamal* hit, the top floor was about the worst place to be. Besides being a man's first name, *shamal* was the name of a strong wind that blew in a huge dust storm once or twice a year, a storm that lasted three or four days. Everything would be normal, with Ishtar learning a lesson or playing a game or swimming in the pool, when suddenly all the servants in the palace would rush in and cover the windows just as the storm hit. Even then much dust made its way into the palace and it took the servants days to clean up.

Ishtar sometimes suspected his tutor could actually conjure up a shamal wind, but today, the only thing on the wind was the secret of Shamal the tutor.

"What?" said Ishtar. "What is your secret?"

Shamal looked around to make sure no one could hear him. "Our current King of Kings is just a bit . . ." Shamal searched for a kind word. "Eccentric," he finally said.

Ishtar's face scrunched into a "huh?" look, but then a moment later took on a look of surprise as he understood. "You mean he's crazy, like Nebuchadnezzar?" he said more loudly than Shamal would have liked.

Shamal nodded his head, then added, "And so all the sub-kings, such as Sheik Konarak, are ignoring him and have almost unlimited power."

Ishtar tried to process this, but a commotion at the door distracted him. Varta ran in pulling Kazeem by the sleeve, and shouted, "Ishtar! You must get ready immediately! Your father has summoned you!"

"For *what*?" Ishtar asked, looking from Varta to Kazeem to Shamal and back again.

"I do not know," Varta said as she pulled Ishtar to his feet. "All I know is you are to be bathed, and dressed in your finest clothes by the fifth bell." The passing of each day was marked by a bell that rang in a tall tower. Some people in the city used it to mark times of prayer. “And you are to see to it!” Varta said to Kazeem.

Twenty minutes later Ishtar had finished the shortest bath he’d ever had and Kazeem saw to it he was dressed in purple silk trousers with gold braiding, a matching purple tunic tied with a gold belt, and a fine wool coat that flowed almost to the floor. Varta then combed his wet hair, which Ishtar insisted he could do himself.

“Ow!” he said as she combed.

“Oh that didn’t hurt,” Varta scolded, and Ishtar wondered how she knew that, though he still pretended to be wounded. As the fifth bell rang out across the city, Kazeem pushed open the towering doors of the throne room, and then propelled Ishtar inside. Ishtar’s eyes almost popped out of his head as he stared at the roomful of the highest nobles, advisors, and teachers of the kingdom, all staring at *him*. Then he saw King Konarak himself, seated on his throne atop a platform at the far end of the room, wearing the royal robes and royal crown of gold. The king stood and moved to the edge of the platform, then shouted for all to hear, “Behold, Prince Ishtar, blessed by the gods, friend to the heavens, counselor and magi to Persia!”

All the nobles, advisors, teachers, and Ishtar’s father and uncles, and even the king himself started applauding so loudly Ishtar thought the walls might fall down. Some of the men began to cheer, and others bowed low.

Ishtar had no idea what was happening, but of one thing he was certain: this was not a dream.

We all have dreams of being rich, or famous, or admired for our talent. And we think we can imagine what it would be like to achieve those dreams. But the truth is that the biggest dreams we can dream are nothing at all compared to the real gifts God wants to give us. Those gifts might not be money, or fame, or popularity, but when they come from God they are always far better, and far more valuable, than anything we can dream up.

> To them God has chosen to make known among the Gentiles the glorious riches of this mystery, which is Christ in you, the hope of glory. COLOSSIANS 1:27

The king has given Ishtar a royal reception for reasons Ishtar doesn't even understand yet. When we put aside our own selfish desires, and allow God to have control of our lives and our works, he can use us in ways we never dreamed possible.

It will feel like a dream come true.

A Mission

Light the first violet candle.

Ishtar had seen chariots before, but never had he touched one, let alone ridden in one. But here he was, standing on the back of the king's own chariot, being pulled by the king's horses and driven by his charioteer, through the main streets of Amaranth. In front of him rode two columns of palace guards, dressed in red and yellow uniforms, each waving a banner and riding a horse. Walking behind him were two columns of priests and nobles, all waving long palm branches, a traditional symbol of goodness. And in front of the whole parade rode trumpeters on horseback, and in another chariot, a *praeco*—a town crier. "Behold how the King treats his most honored servants," the praeco shouted to the city. "Ishtar of Amaranth, Prince of all Persia, friend of the heavens and blessed by the gods, is this day proclaimed to be a Preferred Friend and Advisor to the King!"

Ishtar wasn't sure what he was supposed to do—in fact, he thought, he was *supposed* to be in his etiquette lesson right now—so he just stood on the back of the chariot and waved to the cheering crowds in the market. In all the excitement, he'd missed lunch—something that never happened before except when he was ill—but Ishtar felt only confusion, not hunger.

"Behold how the King treats his most honored servants," the *praeco* repeated. "Ishtar of Amaranth, Prince of all Persia, friend of the heavens and blessed by the gods, is this day proclaimed to be a Preferred Friend and Advisor to the King!"

It had only been an hour earlier that the king had stood in the throne room and said those same words about Ishtar. When at last the applause had died down, the king made an announcement. "Our greatest scientists and trusted officials have examined closely the star that announced itself to Ishtar," he said. Ishtar knew his father and uncles were the scientists and officials the king spoke of, but he had no idea what the last part meant.

"They have calculated," the king continued, "that the appearance of the star signals the imminent fulfillment of an ancient prophecy recorded in many books—the birth of a new and mighty king to our Jewish friends to the west."

This news caught Ishtar by surprise. How could a single star say such a thing?

"I am therefore sending a caravan," the king continued, "to carry gifts to this child, and to honor him as ruler of a friendly nation."

At this a great cheer had gone up in the throne room, and then the king ordered a parade in Ishtar's honor; so now here he was, wondering what in all Persia had just happened.

He continued to wave.

As the parade neared the edge of the city they passed the house of Ishtar's cousins, who were playing in the street. At the sound of the trumpets the cousins looked up and were shocked to see the boy they had played with just the day before being honored in a king's procession. They stared and waved slowly, not believing the sight. Ishtar just waved at them and shrugged his shoulders.

The parade turned another corner and headed back toward the palace down the same market street Ishtar had ridden the day before. Everyone stopped and waved, Ishtar saw, but it seemed like they weren't really very excited about it. In fact, he decided, it looked like they were waving because they had to. Then he saw the same group of boys from the day before. They were waving too, but under their breaths they were chanting, "Mama's boy, mama's boy, mama's boy."

Ishtar looked away in anger and ignored them.

Finally the parade arrived back at the palace and Kazeem led Ishtar back up to his apartment. Varta had a late lunch ready for him, and went on and on about how beautiful it had all been, and how she'd cried as she heard the people cheering him.

Ishtar didn't bother telling her that those cheers weren't very sincere.

"So how does it feel to be a special advisor to the king?"

Ishtar looked up and saw Salamar entering the room, his royal robes billowing behind him.

"Father!" he cried, and gave him a huge hug. "What just happened?"

Salamar laughed loudly. "I guess it swept across you like a shamal wind, did it not?"

"And almost blew me away!" Ishtar answered.

"Well my son, it happened like this." They both sat and Ishtar continued his lunch as Salamar spoke. "The star you discovered last night has never before appeared in the skies. To *anyone*. It's place in the heavens, and the timing of its appearance, signal the birth of a new king, as Sheik Konarak announced."

"But *how*? How can a star say such a thing?"

Salamar shook his head slowly. "It is a very complex question, and requires many calculations and much research for an answer. Some day you will understand, but for now it is enough for you to know this: an event which has been prophesied for a thousand years is about to take place, and your star is going to lead us to that place."

"But I didn't *do* anything!" Ishtar argued. "All I did was look up to answer Alim's question."

Salamar took a deep breath, thinking. "Ishtar," he said at last, "it is not the fact that you saw the star that makes you special. It is the fact that the star chose *you* to appear to!"

Ishtar was still frustrated. "But a star cannot choose or not choose," he said. "A star is just a light in the sky."

A slight smile curved up the corners of Salamar's mouth as he said, "Not *this* star."

Ishtar still didn't understand as Salamar stood and slapped his son on the back. "In any event," he said, "it is clear what the star means, and clear what I must do. You understand, don't you, that I will be leading the caravan the king is sending?"

Ishtar nodded his head sadly. His father had been gone from Amaranth several times during Ishtar's life, leading one expedition or another. Ishtar always hated it—his mother had died giving birth to him, and even though Kazeem and Varta were like family, it wasn't the same. But he understood it was part of his father's duties.

"This will be the longest journey yet," Salamar said, "and will require much preparation."

"How long?" Ishtar asked.

Salamar thought. "At least six months there and back," he said. "Maybe eight."

Ishtar's heart sank. Six months without his father! As much as he loved Kazeem and Varta and all the other servants, there was no one he loved more than his father.

"I must go now and see to preparations," Salamar said, and then was gone.

Ishtar moped around the apartment for a while, thinking about his father being gone. He sat at the edge of the pool and dangled his feet in, but didn't really feel like swimming. There would be little water on his father's journey, he knew. Many caravans had passed through Amaranth, and many caravan leaders had dined at the palace, and the one topic that always came up was water.

And then there were the smells. And the work. And the snakes and winds and . . . Ishtar shuddered as he thought about it, and wondered how his father could stand to take such a trip.

Oh well, he thought at last, it's going to happen and I'd better start planning for it.

Each time his father left on a trip, Ishtar made plans of his own. With six or eight months to work with, he was pretty sure he could cut his lesson times in half. After all, wasn't he Prince of Persia? And now also Special Advisor to the King? And didn't Kazeem, Varta, and all the tutors work for *him*?

So shorter lessons it would be, and maybe no lessons at all in mathematics. He could already add and subtract numbers, and he knew that a homer was ten ephahs of grain, and a cubit was one and a half lengths of a man's foot. What more was there to know? In fact, he decided, instead of lessons every day maybe he should have them only two or three times a week. Ishtar liked that idea best of all.

And then there was bedtime. He never had time to play after astronomy lessons, and always had to leave banquets in the middle if there were no lessons. After his father was gone he'd make bedtime an hour or two later. And *only* after he'd eaten as much dessert as he liked.

Maybe having his father gone for a while wouldn't be so bad after all.

With lessons apparently cancelled for the rest of the day, Ishtar had time to compile a long list of new rules for himself and his servants. No lessons before the third bell of the day, and none after the fifth bell, he decided. Swim times would be any time he wanted. He'd never have to leave the palace, and his cousins could come to play as often as they liked. All through dinner and late into the evening Ishtar kept making plans.

"What's this?" Salamar's voice booming from the darkness startled Ishtar. "My son is actually doing his lessons?"

Ishtar was lying in bed and quickly covered up the wax tablet on which he'd been writing his new rules. "Uh, yes Father, I am, uh, doing much work about my lessons."

Salamar sat on the end of Ishtar's bed. "Ishtar," he said seriously, "you do understand that this will be a very long and very dangerous journey."

Ishtar hadn't thought about the danger before, and now suddenly grew frightened for his father's safety.

"I have ordered a garrison of soldiers to accompany us," Salamar continued, "but even so, there are many thieves and villains who will want the treasure I have been instructed to take to the new king."

"Yes, Father. I understand."

Salamar hugged his son tightly. "Then you understand that Kazeem and Varta will have to care for you in my place."

"Yes, Father," Ishtar said again. This was just like every other trip his father had taken. Kazeem and Varta always stayed home to watch over him.

"But you may see me whenever you wish, and I will still come and settle you in bed each night," Salamar continued.

Ishtar laughed out loud. "Well that's ridiculous!" he said. "How will you put me to bed? Will you fly like a bird back to Amaranth?"

Salamar looked surprised. "What do you mean?"

"I mean . . . I mean how could you put me to bed when you'll be on the caravan and I'll be here in the palace?"

Salamar stared at his son for a long moment. "Ishtar," he said slowly, "I do not think you fully understand the situation. You are going on this journey *with* me!"

Once we allow God to have control of our lives, we might be surprised where he asks us to go.

Ishtar enjoyed being honored, even though he couldn't understand what he did to deserve it. But it never occurred to him that such a reward might come at a price.

God wants to honor us with many gifts, more wondrous than we can imagine. Those gifts are free, and a natural result of following him. But another natural result of following him is that God will give us opportunities and experiences we could never plan for ourselves.

> God's voice thunders in marvelous ways; he does great things beyond our understanding. JOB 37:5

All in all, it's a great, grand adventure of the highest order.

Truant

Light the first violet candle.

Worms of fear had gathered in Ishtar's belly. It had been three days since his father told him he'd be traveling on the caravan across the desert, and for every moment of those three days he'd felt like he was going to throw up. He was scared of the thieves they would meet, scared of the snakes and scorpions that might crawl into his bed, scared of . . . well, scared of everything that wasn't the same as the palace.

And now, sitting in one of the windows of his sleeping chamber, watching dozens of men assembling dozens of camels behind the palace, watching them gather bales of hay, bags of water, and bundles of travel and trading goods, the worms of fear in his belly started squirming even more wildly.

He simply *had* to convince his father to let him stay home.

When his father had told him he'd be going on the caravan, it had taken Ishtar a few moments to understand. At first he thought his father meant he'd accompany the caravan to the edge of the city, and that was bad enough. Then he thought his father meant he'd accompany the caravan to the edge of the province a day's journey away, and that was terrifying. But when he realized his father meant the entire journey, he felt like he'd been slammed in the face by one of the huge palace doors. "But, but you just said I was staying home with Kazeem and Varta!" he'd said. "No, no," his father answered. "I meant that on the journey I will be very busy, and Kazeem and Varta will care for you."

"Well this is just ridiculous!" he said aloud now as he watched an out-of-control camel nip and kick at its handlers. It took three men to force the beast down on its knees so they could calm it and put a muzzle over its snout. "Father will just have to change his mind."

Ishtar hopped down from the window and marched toward the front door of the apartment. "Ishtar! Where are you going?" Kazeem asked.

"To convince my father to allow me to stay home."

Ishtar didn't see the smile on Kazeem's face. "Very well," Kazeem said, and followed his ward.

Salamar's work chamber was on the same floor as the apartment but at the other end of the palace. Ishtar walked quickly down the grand hallway lined with green plants and mosaic-covered walls. Father will listen to logic, he thought. He turned a corner, went down another corridor, then entered Salamar's work chamber. His father worked at a table, his back to the door.

"We'll need another dozen camels for the gifts," he was saying to a much shorter man. Ishtar thought the man looked like he was mean enough to beat a lion in a fight. "And we'd better hire another dozen guards."

"That will mean yet another dozen camels to carry food and water."

"So be it," Salamar said. Ishtar stepped up to the table next to his father. "Ishtar! A nice surprise indeed, but I am very busy."

"Father, I have a most urgent matter to discuss with you," Ishtar said.

Salamar smiled, then turned to the short man. "I trust you to make all necessary arrangements, Rasad," he said. The other man left and Salamar pulled up two stools for Ishtar and himself. "Now, what is this urgent matter?"

Ishtar cleared his throat, then lined up all his thoughts at the front of his brain.

"Well, I've been thinking that, as much as I'd like to go on this journey, it does not seem wise for me to do so."

"And why is that?"

"Well . . ." Ishtar said again. "I know that all of Sheik Konarak's brothers have been killed in various wars . . ."

"Yes, that is so," Salamar said.

"And I know that he has no sons."

"At least not yet," Salamar agreed.

"That means if he were to die of a snake bite or some horrible disease, *you* would become king."

"This is true," Salamar said.

"And if *you* were to die of a snake bite or some horrible disease, *I* would become king, which is why I carry the title of *prince*."

"That is probably true," Salamar said, "but not for certain."

"Well then," Ishtar said, gaining confidence, "it seems to be a poor plan for both you and I to travel in the same caravan across treacherous lands filled with thieves and wild animals. If *both* you and I were killed, there would be no one left to rule over the kingdom!"

Salamar stood and paced. Ishtar didn't see the raised eyebrow and smile his father flashed at Kazeem. "I see you've given this matter much thought," he said finally, "and you are using your logic well."

The worms in Ishtar's belly suddenly vanished and a grin broke out on his face.

"However," Salamar said, and Ishtar's worms returned, "I believe the gods will protect us on our journey, and at least one of us will return safely home. But even if we don't, there are plenty of others in the line of succession to take our place."

Ishtar hung his head in sadness. "Yes, Father," he said. Then he tried a new tactic. "But if I stay home, you won't need as many camels! You won't need camels for my food, for my tents, or my chests of clothing—why, you could probably save a dozen camels right there!"

"Oh, you don't need to worry about that," Salamar said. "We have plenty of camels. Besides, it provides work for the local camel owners."

Ishtar hung his head again, and Salamar patted him on the shoulder. "And consider this," he said softly. "This journey will bring many adventures and many new things to learn, and you and I will get to share them together."

"I don't like adventures. I like knowing exactly what's going to happen."

"Yes, I know, and that may be the best reason to *have* a few adventures. You'll meet many new people and make new friends. If we are fortunate, you will even meet my old friend Nathan from my youth. He once did fifty cartwheels in a row!"

Great, Ishtar thought, *that's just what I want—to meet all your old friends.*

"Now, I must return to my work," Salamar said. "There is still much to do."

"Yes, Father," Ishtar said, and shuffled his way back to the apartment.

"We must make our own preparations for the journey," Kazeem said as they entered the apartment. "They will want to test the load on your camel tomorrow."

Ishtar sat on a Roman-style couch by the pool. "Perhaps *you* could convince Father, Kazeem. A dangerous caravan is no place for a young boy such as myself. And besides, surely *you* don't want to leave all you know and love in Amaranth for such a journey!"

"I serve only you, young master. I go where you go, and I live only to protect you."

Ishtar had never in his life thought about that before, but it was true. Kazeem had no family of his own, no other home, not even a sleeping chamber of his own. From all appearances he was always standing guard just outside whatever room Ishtar was in.

"Now, I must go and select the clothing you will take on the journey," Kazeem said.

"Don't forget to pack my gods," Ishtar said, still pouting. Then he added, "Especially Bes, my protector from snakes!"

All the rest of the day Ishtar pouted. He didn't even feel like eating Varta's zulbia—fried dough dipped in honey and cinnamon. All lessons had been cancelled, so there was nothing else to do but think about the many ways he could be hurt or killed on this silly caravan to visit some baby king in some other country he didn't even care about. But late that night, as he lay in bed, an idea struck Ishtar that he thought was pure genius.

"Ishtar! It is time to arise!" Kazeem called from the curtained entrance to Ishtar's sleeping chamber the next morning.

"Ishtar! Arise!"

Ishtar moaned, but his eyes remained closed. Kazeem took three steps over to the bed and shook Ishtar by the shoulder.

"Ishtar, it is time to wake up!"

But again Ishtar only moaned. That was when Kazeem noticed Ishtar was covered in sweat. He felt the boy's forehead and was shocked. "Child! You burn with fever!" he gasped. "I shall fetch the physician!"

Kazeem ran from the room. The moment he was gone, Ishtar's eyes opened. Sure that he was alone, Ishtar reached down on the far side of his bed where he had hidden an oil lamp heating a wet cloth in a bowl. He quickly dabbed the cloth on his face and over his shoulders and arms. He heard footsteps approaching, dropped the cloth back into the bowl, laid back, and closed his eyes. Half a moment later, Kazeem returned, followed by an old, bald man dressed in robes.

"What did he eat last night?" the old man asked Kazeem.

"Hardly anything. Only a few bites of the same *tabrizi* that I ate."

The physician sat on the bed and examined Ishtar.

"Boy! Open your eyes!" he called, patting Ishtar's face. Ishtar only moaned.

At that moment Salamar ran into the room, out of breath. "What is it?" he gasped. "What's wrong with my son?"

The physician didn't answer for a moment, and instead continued his examination. He raised Ishtar's eyelids one at a time—both eyes were rolled back, a trick Ishtar perfected long ago. He looked in Ishtar's mouth, felt his forehead and cheeks, pressed fingertips to his wrist. Finally he sat up and turned to Salamar.

"Your son is very ill," the physician said, and Salamar's face went white. "It could be the bite of an insect or snake, it could be some bad food he ate, it could even be that some foul enemy has poisoned him. In any case, I fear he is near death."

Ishtar felt his bed jiggle as Salamar, as big and strong as he was, fell to his knees at Ishtar's side. "What can be done?" he asked.

The physician did not answer for several moments. "If I can save him at all, he will require many weeks of bed rest." When the physician said this, Ishtar felt such happiness that he couldn't contain a slight smile but then he quickly straightened his face again. He felt his father's nearness and hoped he hadn't seen.

"Physician," Salamar said slowly, again jiggling the bed as he pulled himself back to his feet, "is there nothing else to be done? Can we not try some leeches? Or perhaps a bit of blood-letting?"

The physician apparently considered that for a moment. Ishtar held his breath. Using leeches to suck the blood from a patient, or even making a small cut in the wrist and allowing it to bleed, were standard medical practices. "Yes, that may indeed be of benefit," the physician said.

"Good," answered Salamar. "Can we begin the treatment immediately?" Ishtar thought his father sounded excited.

"Of course," the physician said. Ishtar heard the sounds of the physician pulling out his tools and his heart began to pound within his chest.

"Be sure you select a very sharp knife," Salamar said loudly. "I want the cut to be very clean."

"Of course," said the physician, sounding a bit annoyed.

"Will this hurt the boy at all?" Salamar asked.

"Not a bit, since he's unconscious," the physician answered. "Of course, if he were awake, it would hurt quite badly."

"Very well," said Salamar. "Proceed."

With that, the physician took Ishtar's wrist in one hand and Ishtar felt the cold of a blade against his skin.

What would you do if you were Ishtar? Would you try to get out of going on the long journey to a foreign place? Would your fear of the unknown make you want to stay home where it's safe and comfortable?

Unfortunately, that's often what we Christians do when God asks us to leave our easy lives and go help others. He has called us to be disciples, to go out into the world and *make* disciples, but we'd rather stay home and do the things that make *us* feel good.

We're such silly children sometimes.

But I'll let you in on a secret: if Ishtar gives in to the authority of his father and willingly faces the hard work ahead, his journey will end in the presence of Jesus.

And I'll let you in on another secret: if *we* give in to the authority of our *heavenly* father, and willingly face the hard work it takes to be a disciple, and to disciple others, our journey will end in exactly the same place.

The Caravan

Light the first violet candle.

Ishtar's eyes suddenly shot open and he jerked his hand away. "No!" he yelled. "Please do not cut me! I am feeling much better!"

The physician was shocked and dropped the knife, then felt the boy's forehead.

"Indeed," he said, "the fever has left and the boy seems quite normal."

"I believe you'll find," Salamar said, looking directly into Ishtar's eyes, "that the boy is completely healed."

The physician packed up his things while mumbling about a miracle of the gods, then left. Salamar nodded at Kazeem, who also stepped out of the room. He sat on the edge of his son's bed and said, "A remarkable recovery."

Ishtar gulped. "Yes, Father."

Salamar leaned over the far side of the bed, then said, "I see you suffered from the oldest disease of small boys."

"What is that, Father?"

"Pretending to be ill to get out of doing that which you do not wish to do."

Ishtar turned his face away, embarrassed.

"Ishtar, to pretend to be ill is to lie. And to lie is the worst of all sins—worse even than making the *poz dadan*."

Ishtar's eyes shot open and his head snapped back toward his father. To make the *poz dadan* was a very bad thing indeed. It meant to boast falsely of one's own accomplishments. If this was even worse . . .

Ishtar began to cry. "I am sorry, Father. I have embarrassed myself, and my household. I shall wear the veil of shame forever."

Salamar patted his son on the shoulder. “All can be forgiven if you are sorry,” he said, “and if you repent.”

Ishtar wiped his eyes, and now realized his plan had failed and he would still have to travel with the caravan. “I . . . I just do not think it wise for me to go on this journey.”

“We’ve already talked about that, Ishtar.”

“Yes, I know,” Ishtar said, sniffling, “but it is just a very bad idea. It . . . it makes no sense! It is a violation of all logic, and a terrible tragedy of error!” Desperate, Ishtar’s shame of a moment before turned into anger. “There is absolutely no reason I should have to go on this journey. I *can’t* go on this journey! I . . . I *won’t* go on this journey!”

Salamar took a deep breath before speaking. “Ishtar, you will do as I say. You *are* coming with me on this caravan, and you will make no more complaint about it. Is that clear?”

Ishtar had heard that tone in his father’s voice before and knew he dare not defy it. He couldn’t get any words to leave his mouth, so simply looked away and nodded. But then his father did something very unexpected: he pulled Ishtar into a hug like a bear protecting its cub.

“Now, my son,” Salamar said, “would you finally like to tell me the truth? Would you like to tell me what you are *really* feeling?”

Ishtar wrapped his arms around his father and began crying again. “I am so afraid!” he said.

“Yes,” Salamar said softly, “finally I hear the truth.”

“I . . . I am afraid of thieves and animals and dying of thirst!”

“I understand,” Salamar said with great sympathy, “and I know your heart. But will you do one thing for me?”

“What?”

“Will you trust that I, and Kazeem, and Varta, your uncles, plus a hundred soldiers and two hundred servants all know what we are doing? That we have done this dozens of times before, and will know how to keep you safe and healthy?”

Ishtar wasn’t sure he could do that, but said nothing more.

“And you can pray to the gods,” Salamar continued.

“Which ones?” Ishtar asked.

“Oh, perhaps the god of camel feet, or the god of sand dunes, or the god of silly fears.”

Ishtar rolled his eyes. "Father, there are no such gods."

Salamar was smiling. "Well then, my friend Nathan is quite adamant that there is only *one* God. Perhaps you could pray to him."

"That's ridiculous!" Ishtar said seriously, even though he knew his father was just trying to get him to laugh. "How could there be only one god?"

"I will leave you to figure that out for yourself," Salamar said, standing. "But for now, I have much work to do."

"Must I take my daily lessons on this journey?" Ishtar asked.

"No, your tutors will not be going with us," Salamar answered. "But you are sure to learn many hundreds of lessons. Maybe thousands." Ishtar was happy he wouldn't have to listen to his tutors drone on and on, but suspected that whatever his father meant was going to be far worse. That seemed to be the way with adults.

Ishtar did indeed try praying to the gods about the catastrophe facing him. As usual, they didn't seem to be listening. Three days later Kazeem woke him early in the morning, long before the sun rose. "Ishtar! Awake! It is time."

Ishtar rubbed his eyes and tried to open them, but his brain really wanted to go back to sleep. What was Kazeem talking about? Then he remembered and sat straight up. "Oh no!" he yelled. Kazeem smiled, but Ishtar knew there was nothing to smile about.

"Eat well, young master," Varta said. "It will be your last breakfast for many days."

What does she mean by that? Ishtar wondered. He'd had a fine breakfast every morning of his life and he wasn't about to stop now. Of course *this* breakfast would be much better if it weren't for the noise of the camels out behind the palace.

It was still dark outside, and would be for a few hours yet. All the torches and lamps around the apartment and pool were lit as if ready for a party. Ishtar could see no cause for celebration. But as he took a bite of some flatbread fresh off the grill and smothered it with sweet pomegranate jam, he decided that maybe he should change his attitude and make the best of this journey. After a bite of *reshteh khoshkar*—a rice pastry soaked in syrup then covered in cinnamon and nuts—he decided that, yes, this was a good idea. He would change his attitude and enjoy this journey. He washed that thought down with the last of his tea.

After breakfast Ishtar washed, then put on the clean jacket Kazeem had laid out for him. "Kazeem, you have packed all my trunks, correct?"

Kazeem gave Ishtar a strange look then said, "I have packed your clothes exactly as your father ordered."

"Good, then let us go down. I am anxious to get started."

Ishtar didn't see the look of surprise Kazeem gave Varta, but they followed their charge out the door and down the stairs to the courtyard. Ishtar stopped and looked around, confused. "Kazeem!" he called. "Where are my bearers? And where is my *tahtirevan*?"

Kazeem knelt next to Ishtar and spoke softly. "Young master, perhaps I have not properly prepared you for this journey."

Ishtar was annoyed. "There will be time for that later. Now where are my bearers?"

Kazeem cleared his throat. "Ishtar," he said, "there will be no bearers, and no *tahtirevan*. This is a *caravan*. Except for a few soldiers on horseback, everyone walks, or rides a camel. There are no exceptions."

Ishtar's eyes grew wide. "A *camel!*" he said in disgust. "I cannot ride a camel! They stink! And they're mean!"

Kazeem stood and shrugged. "Well then, I guess you will walk."

Ishtar's head spun as Kazeem and Varta led him out the back door of the palace.

He had to *walk*? All the way to Palestine? This was ridiculous. He'd have to talk to his father immediately.

The noise of the camels was almost unbearable. They were being loaded with the bales and bags and bundles. As the heavy loads were lifted onto their backs, the camels complained loudly with a sort of screaming growl that sounded like a mule, a cow, and a sheep all put together. They were so loud that Ishtar had trouble thinking the angry thoughts he was tying to think.

With Varta in front of him and Kazeem behind, Ishtar trudged through the sand up the long line of camels, holding his nose. Suddenly Varta stopped, so Ishtar did too. "This is yours," Kazeem said.

Ishtar was confused for a moment, then saw that Kazeem was pointing at a camel. "You may ride him or not," Kazeem said, "but he is a young animal, and will be a good steed for you if you so choose."

Ishtar stared at the camel. He didn't know much about the animals, but he knew that some camels have one hump and some have two. This one—and all the others in the caravan—had two. Unlike most the other camels, this one carried no load, only an ornate saddle of wood and leather between the humps. He had shaggy hair on his four legs, making it look as though he was wearing trousers, a thick, shaggy mane on his neck running from his mouth down to his chest, and a shaggy plop of hair on top of his head that looked like a hat. The camel stared back for a moment, then opened his mouth and spit on Ishtar's coat.

"Yuck!" Ishtar cried and jumped back. "Get that dirty thing away from me!" He tried to wipe the spit off with his hand but the coat was soaked. "Kazeem, fetch me a fresh coat," Ishtar ordered.

Just then the clang of two bells being struck with a stick sounded from the front of the caravan. One bell was lower in tone than the other, and they were being struck in rapid succession. "What is that?" Ishtar asked. Before anyone could answer, the long line of camels suddenly lurched forward and started moving. "Quickly, Kazeem, a clean coat!"

Kazeem, Varta, Ishtar, and everyone else were now walking alongside the caravan. "There is no clean coat for you," Kazeem said.

"What! You said you packed my clothes!"

"I said I packed exactly what your father told me to pack. Two pair of trousers, two tunics, one coat, and one set of fine clothes for when you meet the king."

Ishtar stared up at his bodyguard. "You mean I can only have clean clothes once each day?"

Kazeem shook his head. "No, Ishtar. You may only have clean clothes once each week or two, when we have time and opportunity to wash and bathe."

Ishtar was in such shock and disbelief that he didn't even notice the torches of the palace fading behind them as they slowly marched away from everything he'd ever known. He did notice in the sky in front of them the star, and wished now he had never discovered it.

A few hours later the sun rose in the sky behind the caravan and the star disappeared. Ishtar had only seen a sunrise a few times in his life, and now was curious about his own long shadow that tripped off his feet, mimicking his every step. Those feet were already sore, tired, and dusty, and his stomach was asking for a proper lunch.

And that's when Ishtar did something that almost destroyed the caravan.

Following God isn't always easy. We may have to give up some of the luxuries of life that we're used to.

Ishtar was shocked that he'd have to walk on this journey, instead of being carried. He was shocked to learn he'd have to ride a camel, and wouldn't be able to swim and have clean clothes every day. He'd gotten so used to his life in the palace that he couldn't imagine giving it up.

Maybe we have also become used to our easy lives. What would we do if God asked us to leave all that behind and walk with him? Would we be willing to walk away from it all to do that which God asks us to do? Would we willingly obey, and follow him without question?

> To this you were called, because Christ suffered for you, leaving you an example, that you should follow in his steps. 1 PETER 2:21

Error of Judgment

Light the first violet candle.

Ishtar's feet were sore from walking, and the rumblings in his stomach were starting to hurt. He'd been walking next to the camel assigned to him since long before sunrise. He tried to keep several arms' lengths to its left, though, because it stunk so bad.

In the daylight Ishtar could see ahead of them some cliffs rising from the sands, and he hoped they wouldn't be climbing those. Here, still close to the sea, there was enough rain during the year for green plants and even a few trees to grow. On top of those cliffs, he knew, was a strange land with no water.

Kazeem was walking three camels behind Ishtar, talking with Varta. Ishtar stopped and let them catch up, then fell in pace next to them. His two servants were in deep discussion about something Ishtar didn't understand.

"Kazeem, where is the food carried?" he asked.

With his mind still on his conversation with Varta, Kazeem answered absently. "The first two beasts carry your food and water," he said, "the third is yours to ride, and the other five carry the rest of our belongings and fodder for the animals themselves."

Ishtar analyzed the answer as Kazeem went back to his conversation. He saw now that the entire caravan was made up of strings of eight camels, with a rope tied from the saddle of one camel to the neck harness of the one behind it, and so forth. It seemed that he had a string all his own, managed by Kazeem, Varta, and another man, and that others took care of other strings.

"I will have my lunch now," Ishtar announced to his two servants. They both looked at Ishtar in surprise as they continued walking. "Ishtar," Varta said, "lunch is not taken until the bells ring."

Well that's ridiculous, Ishtar thought. And then he decided he'd just have to find lunch for himself.

Kazeem had said that Ishtar's food and water were being carried by the first two camels in his string, so he walked faster until he reached them.

The thought of getting nearer the animals, let alone touching them, almost made Ishtar lose his appetite, but he decided that having lunch would be worth the risk. After several tries he finally held his nose and forced himself to get close to the camel.

The camel's load was bound up in large bundles wrapped in cloth and rope, one bundle hanging on each side and one on top. Ishtar couldn't tell which bundle held the food, so he'd just have to search. A knot in the rope holding the closest bundle hung inches from his face, so he reached up and gave the knot a tug. It wouldn't budge, so he pulled harder. Still the knot refused to release. Ishtar decided he'd have to work at the knot, but it was difficult with the animal swaying back and forth as it walked.

"Well this is ridiculous!" Ishtar said aloud. Then he walked to the front of the camel, grabbed the rope hanging from its harness, and gave it a hard pull.

"Whoa!" he said, as he'd heard many riders say to their horses.

"Ishtar! No!" It was Kazeem, who now came running up the line. But it was too late. The camel obeyed Ishtar's command and stopped dead in its tracks. The next camel in line bumped the first before stopping, and the bundle Ishtar had loosened fell open, spilling hundreds of pounds of goods onto the sand. Now all the camels in Ishtar's string came to a halt. The camels following Ishtar's string, however, didn't stop. Some of them turned to the side and headed away from the caravan. Some of them seemed to go mad and bucked and screamed. All down the long line, for as far as Ishtar could see, there was chaos and camels.

"Ishtar! What have you done?" Kazeem yelled.

Ishtar began to cry. "I . . . I was just trying to get something to eat!" he said.

Next came Salamar riding fast on his camel. "What hap . . ." he said, but stopped, having figured it out. He looked down on the sight with his mouth hanging open.

Before he could say any more, another man came riding up. "What's going on here? Who stopped the caravan?" Ishtar saw that it was the short, stout man he'd seen in his father's office. He was red in the face as he jumped down from his camel and stomped over to the scene.

"Who is responsible for this mess?"

Everyone stared at Ishtar, who could only say, "I . . . I . . ."

"Rasad," Salamar said, addressing the short man, "it matters little who is at fault. What is important now is to get moving again."

"What's important is for *discipline* to be maintained! What's *important* is for our schedule to be kept! I am the *karvan-salar*, and I alone will determine what is important! And I can tell you there will be punishment for this tonight!"

Rasad was still red in the face and breathing heavily, but his rage had been deflated by his tirade. He looked at the mess again, yelled, "Now clean this up!" then returned to his camel and started giving orders to get the caravan moving again.

Salamar sighed and dismounted his camel. "Come," he said to the others, "let us repack this camel." Ishtar was shocked when he realized "us" included him.

It took almost three hours to round up all the camels, settle them down, and get them back in line, and to repack the many loads that had been loosened in the fray. "Why are the camels all so grumpy?" Ishtar asked his father as they worked.

"Caravans travel all day without stopping," Salamar answered, "and as soon as they do stop for the night, the camels are fed and watered. So when you stopped them, that's what they expected."

With the whole company moving again, Salamar pulled Ishtar up to sit in front of him on his camel. "Come," he said, "let us have a lesson in caravanning." Ishtar held his nose against the stench. They trotted up the line toward the front and Salamar said, "Tell me what you have observed."

Ishtar thought for a moment. "I have observed that camels are tied together nose-to-tail in strings of eight," he said. "And that there is one man in charge of each string."

"Correct," Salamar answered. "Each of these strings is called a 'file,' and the man in charge is known as a camel-puller. We have sixty-two files, so how many camels is that?"

Ishtar calculated in his head then answered, "Four hundred ninety-six."

"Excellent."

"Why such a big caravan just to carry a few gifts?" Ishtar asked.

"Many reasons." Salamar's low voice, almost a whisper, tickled Ishtar's ear. "First, there are many dangers in the desert—thieves, sandstorms, wild animals. There is safety in numbers. Second, we carry a wealth of gifts for the new king, not just a few trinkets. Gold, frankincense, myrrh—all very valuable. So we need many soldiers to guard the wealth. And third—well, it wouldn't be a very impressive tribute to have just your two uncles and me ride up on three shaggy camels, now would it? A tribute to a king must *look* like a tribute."

Ishtar looked behind him at the line of camels extending clear back over the farthest hill and decided this was, indeed, an impressive caravan.

"Which camels carry the gold, frankincense, and myrrh?" he asked.

His father looked around quickly. "Hush! Do not talk of this aloud. Only a few people even know we carry such wealth." Satisfied that no one had heard the comment, he turned to Ishtar and said, "I do not know where they are. They are hidden throughout the caravan so that a thief cannot simply steal one camel and so get our entire fortune. Only Rasad knows where the gifts are packed."

"Who is Rasad?"

Salamar took a deep breath before answering. "He is the *karvan-salar*—the leader of this caravan."

"I thought *you* were the leader," Ishtar said.

"I am the leader of the mission," Salamar answered, "but we hired Rasad to lead the caravan itself. He is an experienced *karvan-salar*. He knows the route to take, the location of every village and oasis. He can read the ripples in the sand and know exactly where we are, and how to get where we are going. We would be lost without him, and he is in absolute control of everything that happens in the caravan. He's also the man who was so upset when you stopped us unexpectedly."

Ishtar thought for a moment. "You mean the small man?"

"I would not say he is small," Salamar answered. "He is far bigger in many ways than most men I know. And he's built like a bear!"

Then a horrible thought struck Ishtar. "What did Rasad mean when he said there would be punishment for stopping the caravan?"

Salamar was silent for a moment, then said, "The *karvan-salar* is in absolute control as I said. Each evening he holds court for various infractions that happen during the day's journey. And then he inflicts punishment."

Ishtar gulped. "What sort of punishment?"

"Well, it can be anything, from loss of a meal, to a whipping, to banishment from the caravan, or, in very serious cases, death."

And at that, Ishtar began to tremble.

Ishtar was only thinking of himself when he stopped the caravan, and thinking only of yourself can have terrible consequences.

Sometimes it's really hard to put the needs and desires of others ahead of our own. If we don't look out for ourselves, who will look out for us?

The answer is that God has promised to *always* care for us, and be with us through every need, desire, and situation.

Ishtar has not yet learned to trust that his father, Kazeem, and Varta will take care of him. The sooner *we* learn to trust that *God* is watching out for us, the sooner we'll be able to live an unselfish life that he can both bless and use.

But I trust in you, O LORD; I say, "You are my God." PSALM 31:14

The Substitute

Light the first violet candle.

All Ishtar could think about was the punishment to come. When Ishtar asked why he couldn't travel with his father's file of camels at the front of the caravan, Salamar answered, "It is far too dangerous. Rasad and I have calculated that you are safest where we have put you, in the middle of the pack." Ishtar hung his head. "But do not worry, my son. Once we stop each day I shall see you for the third meal."

Kazeem reached them, and together he and Ishtar waited for Ishtar's file of camels to catch up. "Do you wish to walk, or do you wish to ride?" Kazeem asked.

"I'll walk," said Ishtar, and he trudged through the sand amidst dozens of other servants, soldiers, and officials.

When the sun was straight overhead the two bells at the front of the caravan rang again and everyone seemed to perk up. "It's lunch time," Kazeem said, and Ishtar got excited. He had been wondering how they would eat while walking, but decided the most efficient way would be to have each servant carry one type of food and take it around to the other travelers. He was confused, then, when only Varta from his own file started preparing lunch. He watched as she lifted a pouch with a long neck off the lead camel and put it over her shoulder. She then took a wooden cup out of a bundle. She opened the pouch and poured a dirty white slop into the cup and drank it.

Next she went to the camel-puller and gave him some.

Ishtar got a sick feeling in his stomach. He watched as one after another each of the people around him got one cup of the awful-looking gruel. Finally Varta came over to Ishtar. "Now you have seen how it works," she said. "It is your turn. In future days, I will feed you first." She held the cup out for him.

"I will not eat that!" he said.

Varta looked at Kazeem, who said, "Yes, he will."

"Kazeem," Ishtar whined, "I cannot eat that . . . that . . ."

"It is called *millet*, Ishtar. And you *must* eat it. You *will* eat it."

"You cannot give me orders!" Ishtar snapped. Kazeem gave him a long, stern look, and Ishtar wavered. Finally he took the cup from Varta, sniffed at it, and scrunched up his nose. "It stinks!" he said.

"Then I suggest you do not smell it," Varta said gently, "but you *must* eat it. Without proper nourishment you will die out here."

Ishtar stared at the slimy looking mush, stuck his tongue in to taste it, then finally gulped the entire cup down in one turn. It was cold and slimy and left grit in his mouth.

"There, now that wasn't so bad," Kazeem said as he took his own cup of millet.

Ishtar was still trying to chew up the grit and get the taste out of his mouth. "Why can we not have a proper meal?"

Kazeem sighed. "Look around you, Ishtar. Can you not understand we are many people, and will be traveling many months? We cannot possibly carry cakes and fruits and meats."

"So we have to eat millet for lunch every day?" Ishtar asked.

"No," Kazeem answered. "We eat it for lunch, for breakfast, and for most dinners."

Ishtar gasped, and began to wonder if this new king of the Jews would really be worth all this suffering.

Later that afternoon there was a commotion, and people started looking and pointing off to the right of the caravan. "What is it?" Ishtar asked. "What's going on?"

"Bandits," Kazeem said with disgust in his voice. "They are trying to decide if it is worth it to attack us."

Ishtar looked again and finally saw a group of men on horses far off toward the horizon. For the rest of the day Ishtar kept looking over his shoulder expecting an attack at any time. But none came, and soon such events were just part of the daily routine.

Shortly after the sun set over the hills in front of the caravan the two bells rang once again. As if they had practiced, all the files of camels began to form a large circle and Ishtar decided that these people must have done this many times before.

In an amazingly short amount of time, the camels were unloaded, tents were set up, and fires were started. Kazeem led Ishtar up to his father's tent, a large and colorful structure of lightweight silk held up by tall poles. It didn't surprise Ishtar at all that the floor was covered in fine rugs, or that the tent had a large dining area and smaller rooms along the sides. He hugged his father and said, "Which sleeping chamber is mine?"

Salamar frowned. "You will not be staying in my tent," he said. "Kazeem has prepared one of your own, back next to your file."

"But *why*," Ishtar cried. "I want to be with you!"

Salamar was slow to answer. "It is the way it must be," he said, and Ishtar felt a stab of pain in his heart. He was about to argue when Rasad appeared. He stood in the doorway with his fists on his waist and a whip in his hand.

"It is time for the hearings and punishment," he said sternly, and Ishtar nearly wet himself.

Salamar looked at Rasad. "*Karvan-salar*, there is no need to punish the boy. He made an innocent mistake borne of ignorance."

"There are no innocent mistakes on a caravan," Rasad snapped, "and ignorance is not an excuse. The boy's foolishness cost us hours of travel. We should be on top of the plateau already, but we are too late to climb the mountain in the daylight, and we cannot climb it in the dark. Our first day of travel, and already we are half a day behind! The boy will be punished!"

Salamar had handled many diplomatic negotiations in his day and now put on his best negotiating voice. "Surely, Rasad, my friend, you must demonstrate your strength and resolve to the rest of the caravan. I understand that completely. But sometimes the strength of a leader is best shown in his mercy."

"Mercy is for the weak," Rasad snapped again. "These camel-pullers and servants respect only strength. The strength of the whip, not of words."

"Your own King David wrote in a song, 'The Lord has heard my cry for mercy; the Lord accepts my prayer.'"

"Yes," Rasad answered, "but I am not Jehovah, and this is not Jerusalem."

"Perhaps a substitute then. Your Torah allows for a substitute sacrifice."

This remark made the *karvan-salar* pause. "You know us well," he said.

"I once had a seven-year debate about your god with a good friend."

"Very well, a substitute. But no animals. We cannot spare them."

Salamar nodded slowly. "Then I must bare my own back to the whip and take the punishment for my son," he said. "For it is I who failed to properly teach and prepare the boy for caravan life."

"No, Father!" Ishtar yelled. Kazeem stepped forward and held him tightly.

Rasad looked back and forth between Salamar and Ishtar. "So be it! Follow me!" Then he turned and stomped out of the tent.

Rasad led them to the main campfire where all the caravan except for some guards were gathered. Already on the first day there had been a fight over food and another over a perceived insult. Rasad heard both cases and made swift judgments—the loss of a meal in the first case and in the second the two offenders would be bound together at the wrist for three days, or until they could learn to respect each other.

Finally it was Ishtar's turn. "There is no evidence to be heard in this case," Rasad said loudly enough to be heard across the crowd. "The circumstances are clear, and the judgment is made. For selfish actions that led to the stopping of the caravan and great risk for all, the punishment shall be five lashes of the whip. The guilty one will step forward."

All eyes turned to Ishtar, who was crying and still held by Kazeem. But the entire crowd gasped as Salamar stepped forward and removed his tunic. The great man turned his back to the *karvan-salar* and stood firm saying, "Let the punishment fall on me."

Rasad uncoiled the whip and gave it a test snap, which made everyone jump.

Ishtar was hysterical now, seeing in his mind the whip cutting into the flesh of his father. Rasad squared his body behind Salamar, set his feet in the sand, and drew his arm back to strike. But then he wavered and lowered his arm. Twice more he raised the whip, ready to deliver the punishment, only to drop it again. Finally he walked up and growled in Salamar's ear. "I cannot punish a noble one for the crime of another!" he said.

"And I cannot allow you to inflict punishment on one whom it would destroy. If your lash demands justice, Rasad, then it must find it on *my* back. You will not harm my child."

Rasad stepped back and cleared his throat, then yelled, "You see how royalty faces punishment?" He looked around at the faces gathered in the firelight. "Do you see how a noble one bears the guilt of the weak, though he himself be innocent?" He scrambled for some words to say, then finally blurted out, "Now let this be a lesson to you and do not forget that my authority on this caravan is absolute!"

With that he coiled up the whip and quickly walked back into his tent.

Ishtar was still in tears as he looked around at the people leaving. "What happened?" he asked his father.

Salamar shrugged. "I guess Rasad decided he really *could* show mercy for innocent errors."

Ishtar almost collapsed in relief, and vowed to stay far away from the *karvan-salar* for the rest of the journey.

Salamar and Ishtar, along with Bozan, Jodhpur, and some of their advisors, returned to Salamar's tent where a fine dinner had been set. "Do not get used to this, Ishtar," his father warned. "Most nights it will be millet for dinner. But this close to home, I arranged a hearty meal to be brought out for the entire caravan."

After dinner, Kazeem led Ishtar back to the small tent he'd set up for the boy. Ishtar started to enter but Kazeem pulled him back. "You must never enter your tent until I have checked it," he said. "All manner of evil can hide behind these flaps."

Ishtar nodded, then entered after Kazeem said it was clear. "There's not even room to stand up and change clothes!" Ishtar complained.

"It is good, then, that you will not often have clothes to change," Kazeem said.

Ishtar frowned but said nothing. At least he had a soft bed of blankets on which to lay his exhaustion. But then he discovered it wasn't as soft as it looked.

Just as he closed his eyes, there was a noise at the tent flap and Ishtar grabbed his blanket in fright.

"Is Ishtar of Persia ready to sleep?"

"Father!" Ishtar grinned at Salamar's head poking into his tent. "You have come to say goodnight?"

"I told you, my son, that nothing will prevent me from settling you in bed each night."

Ishtar's grin turned to a frown. "I still do not understand why I cannot stay in your tent."

"Oh, camel spit!" Salamar said with a wave of his hand, dismissing the thought. "You would not like it at all. I snore."

Salamar and Ishtar prayed to the gods for safety and good sleep, then Salamar kissed Ishtar on the forehead and departed.

As Kazeem started to lash the door of the tent closed, Ishtar stopped him. "Kazeem, what my father said, about me not staying in his tent. It is because of thieves, correct?"

Kazeem hesitated, then said, "Yes, it is so. If thieves attack in the night they will look for riches, and young princes to kidnap, in the large tents of your father and uncles. Your father protects you by giving you this small tent far from his own."

Ishtar thought for a moment, then said simply, "Good night, Kazeem."

"Good night, my young master. May the gods grant you wondrous sleep, for I will be watching just outside."

But as Ishtar lay his head on his pillow, his fears kept him from sleep—fears full of thieves and mad camels and the *karvan-salar*. His greatest fear, though, was that his fears were not big enough to fear the many things that were to come.

Rasad's law demanded that someone be punished for Ishtar's mistake, and such is the way of laws. They exist to keep us safe, but that means they also exist to punish us if we do wrong.

But Salamar knew his son could not survive the punishment of the law, so he stepped in to take Ishtar's place. Though he was innocent, he was ready to take the sins of his son on himself.

And that's exactly why Jesus came to earth.

Before Jesus, we humans lived under the laws of God, and the punishment of that law was harsh. But God, our Father, knew we couldn't survive that punishment. So he sent his own Son to take our sins upon himself. He took our punishment, so that we wouldn't have to. Our punishment would have been death, but now we can have life instead.

> For the law was given through Moses; grace and truth came through Jesus Christ.
>
> JOHN 1:17

When Rasad saw that Salamar was ready to suffer Ishtar's punishment, he decided the law had been satisfied and extended mercy to them both.

God's mercy is a good thing to celebrate at Christmas.

Peril

Light the first two violet candles.

Ishtar had barely closed his eyes in sleep, it seemed, before Kazeem shook him awake. "Arise, young master. It is a new day!" But the darkness Ishtar saw through the flap of the tent told him it was still very much night.

Ishtar yawned and stretched. Everything from his ears to his toenails hurt from the previous day's walking. Then he almost gagged when he saw Varta approaching him with a cup of millet. Harsh words of complaint started to form in his mouth, but then he remembered that his father had almost been whipped the night before because of Ishtar's own actions, and he decided it would be more prudent to hold his nose and gulp the slop. Just as he lifted the cup to his mouth Kazeem's giant hand snatched it from him.

"Kazeem! That's my *breakfast!*" he squealed.

The bodyguard looked carefully at the cup. "Just as I feared," he said. "This millet is spoiled. It would be deadly to one who eats it."

Shaking, with terror in her eyes, Varta took the cup. "How did you know?" Kazeem pointed to some bubbles in the millet. Varta shook her head slowly, staring at the cup. "I shall borrow some fresh millet from another file," she said.

Servants, Varta, and Kazeem began rolling up sleeping pads, folding up tents, and packing cooking gear. "You know," Kazeem said to Ishtar, "another pair of hands working would make this go much faster."

At first Ishtar was shocked at the suggestion that he help in such menial tasks, but then he looked across the camp and saw that every man and woman was helping in the work, including his father and uncles. And he remembered how everyone had helped clean up his mess the first day. So with a sigh of resignation he began rolling and folding and packing, Kazeem teaching him along the way.

The two bells rang, and the caravan lurched forward. This time Ishtar knew they would not stop until the sun had once again set. As they started up the narrow path into the steep cliffs, Ishtar understood why the caravan could not have climbed them in the dark. He was amazed the animals could even fit on the trail, let alone climb up it with a load.

"Come, it will be safer for you on your camel," Kazeem said. Without waiting for a reply, he lifted Ishtar up to the saddle. From here Ishtar could not see the trail below, only the cliff's sheer drop to his right.

"Kazeem! What are you doing?" he shouted, wrinkling his nose at the smell of the camel. "I will surely fall to my death!"

"The camel will not miss a step on this steep and rocky trail," Kazeem said. "I have no such confidence in your own feet. You are much safer up there."

Sure enough, shortly after the sun reached the noon hour, Ishtar's camel safely reached the top of the trail and followed the files in front of it out onto the flat.

The heat punched Ishtar in the face. He sucked in great breaths, and felt like he was suffocating.

"Kazeem," he called weakly, "I cannot breath!"

"Breath through your nose, little one," Kazeem said. Then he pulled out Ishtar's black wool coat and threw it over the boy's head and shoulders.

"Are you trying to roast me like a pig?" Ishtar shouted.

"The wool blocks the sun the best," Kazeem answered, "and the dark color pulls the heat away from your body. It holds in your moisture during the heat of the day, and holds in your heat in the cold of night."

Sure enough, though covered in wool, it acted more like a shelter than a blanket and Ishtar felt much cooler. After several hours of riding, the camel didn't smell as bad either.

"What is this place?" Ishtar asked, looking at an endless flat plain with no trees or grass.

"This is the high plateau of Zagros. It will take many weeks to cross, and many more to recover from its crossing."

A short time later Ishtar looked around and saw that everyone else in the caravan had also shaded themselves in wool, and that they now climbed onto the backs of camels. Soon there was no one left walking, not even Kazeem. Ishtar was so hungry he was actually happy to see the cups of millet being passed around for lunch.

As the sun set that evening they arrived at their first oasis—a small pond surrounded by palm trees. The pond was too salty to drink, but there was a well and they paid the owners five sacks of grain for the right to refill their water bags. "A generous amount," Salamar said. "For a caravan this size you should never pay more than five sacks of grain for water."

It was while they were setting up the tents—Kazeem had taught Ishtar how to pound the stakes into the ground and Ishtar enjoyed it—that Ishtar saw a dark figure head into the desert, away from the oasis. He could not see the person, but wondered why anyone would go into the night alone.

Around the campfire a short time later, Salamar called for silence. "I have two announcements," he said, sitting atop his camel to be heard. "First, there is another caravan approaching from the north and east. They will arrive shortly and camp to the north. We have made contact with them, and they are a friendly group of traders from Chola. Tomorrow, you may bargain with them as you wish. Second," he continued, "from this point on we must be guided directly by the star. Therefore, we shall be traveling only at night."

Everyone started talking at once, some excited, some concerned. Ishtar heard some say traveling at night would be much cooler and faster. Others worried they would stumble in the darkness, or fail to see a snake or scorpion in their path. Salamar clapped his hands loudly and everyone was instantly silent.

"I know that night travel is both good and bad, but for us it is the only option. We will therefore rest here tonight and all day tomorrow, and continue our journey tomorrow night as soon as the star appears. I suggest," Salamar concluded his speech, "that you stay awake as long as possible tonight, and sleep tomorrow, to prepare yourselves for the weeks ahead."

The crowd started to disperse and Ishtar ran up to Salamar. "Father! Father! Does this mean I may stay up all night?"

Salamar smiled. "Yes, if you can. But you are still under the care of Kazeem, and he will decide when you are to sleep." Ishtar jumped up and down in a cheer. "But first," Salamar continued, "you, your uncles, and I have been invited to dine with the traders from the other caravan. You will wash, and dress in your formal clothes."

Ishtar cheered again at the thought of this. He ran back to his own tent with Kazeem on his heels. "Kazeem! I get to put on clean clothes!"

"Ishtar! Slow down!" Kazeem yelled.

"I shall look like a prince again!"

"Slow down, I said!"

Ishtar ignored his bodyguard. He ran up to his tent, dropped to his knees and crawled through the door flap as Kazeem yelled, *"Ishtar NO!"*

Ishtar froze as if every bone and muscle in his body had turned to rock. Only inches away, a pair of green eyes stared him in the face. But they were not human eyes, and as his own eyes adjusted to the light he saw the gaping mouth, fangs, and spread hood of a king cobra.

Ishtar didn't blink, but he did utter the slightest bit of a whimper. The cobra was also still, exactly as Ishtar had seen in the many snake-charmer shows that had come through Amaranth. He knew the cobra was always most still just before it struck.

Then the cobra twitched ever so slightly and lunged toward Ishtar's throat. In that same moment a powerful hand grabbed Ishtar by the back of the tunic and pulled him into the air as a long, curved, sword sliced through the wall of the tent and cut off the head of the snake.

Ishtar landed several feet back as Kazeem made sure the serpent was dead. Now that the danger was past he began to scream and scramble away in the dirt. Kazeem dropped to his side. "Ishtar, it is over. You are safe." But Ishtar broke down crying and hugged Kazeem tightly. "You have had a terrible fright," the bodyguard said, "but all is well." Then he pulled away and looked Ishtar in the eyes. "This is why you must always do as I say! There are many dangers in the desert, and many of them would love to eat you."

Ishtar calmed a little and nodded. "I am thankful you were close by." A moment later he added, "Why did my god Bes not protect me?"

By the time word came that the other caravan had arrived, Ishtar had recovered from the encounter, had washed in buckets of well water and put on his formal clothes. They were more wrinkled than he'd like, but he decided that was to be expected when traveling.

Kazeem escorted Ishtar to Salamar's tent. "I will leave him in your care. I have some repairs to attend to," Kazeem said to Salamar.

"Oh? Is there trouble I should know about?"

Kazeem looked at Ishtar, then back at his employer. "No, nothing serious. Just some minor cleaning and repairs to Ishtar's tent."

Kazeem left and Ishtar was happy to be with his father. As they walked toward the other caravan he said, "I believe Kazeem is a very good bodyguard. Do we pay him enough?"

Salamar was confused. "Why . . . yes, we pay him well. Ishtar, what happened?"

But by then they had reached the large, ornate tent of the traders. They removed their sandals and stepped onto thick, soft rugs. The tent was huge, with oil lamps hanging from the poles. A full banquet had already been set and Ishtar wondered how they managed that in the short time since they'd arrived.

Ishtar was introduced to the sheik whose tent this was, several traders, and some other men whose names he'd never remember. Salamar offered a gift of tea to the Sheik, then they all sat on pillows and began the casual conversation that was strictly regulated by culture and tradition. For every one thing a man might say, the responder had to choose carefully between eight or ten possible answers or risk offending the other.

Salamar was carefully negotiating such a conversation with the other men, speaking of politics, families, history, and business. Ishtar wasn't really listening, though, because he kept seeing the cobra staring him in the face, and thinking about how it got into his tent.

That's why he didn't hear when the conversation turned to religion. Through the mist of his own thoughts he heard someone say, "But of course, there exists only *one* god."

Ishtar let out a loud laugh. "Well *that's* ridiculous!" he yelled.

Every man seated around the dinner sucked in his breath. Salamar stared at his son wide-eyed. The sheik—who had made the comment—sat with his mouth open.

And five of the sheik's men jumped to their feet, drew their swords, and pointed them directly at Ishtar and his father.

Ishtar is old enough to know better than to ignore the warning yell of an adult, but young enough to *forget* to obey such a warning. It almost got him killed.

That's why adults watch out for children, and teach them to obey even when they don't understand why.

It's like that with God, too. Some of us are old enough—have been around God long enough—to know how he wants us to behave. But then we get excited with our own plans, or see an attractive opportunity, and run off chasing it, leaving God far behind and ignoring his warnings.

Giving up control of our lives to God is tough. But submission to God is what brings us true life.

The Debate

Light the first two violet candles.

Ishtar felt as if he were looking into the face of the cobra again. Everyone was still, everyone was staring at him, and five long, wide, curved swords were pointed at his throat like fangs. He instantly knew he'd done a terrible thing, but it took several moments before he knew how to fix it. Salamar was about to say something when finally Ishtar's training took over.

"Your majesty," Ishtar said, bowing his head to the sheik. "I beg your forgiveness. My remark was rude and insulting. Not only did I speak when only elders should be speaking, but I spoke unkind words in an unkind manner to another in his own tent. I have shamed my father, my teachers, and my people, and I beg your pardon."

Ishtar bowed his head low to the ground and waited. There were many long moments of silence as the sheik stared, a piece of meat halfway to his mouth. Finally he raised one hand and the swords withdrew. Then he spoke.

"And why do you call the idea of only one god ridiculous?" he asked.

Ishtar raised his head slowly, then looked at his father.

"The sheik has asked you a question directly," Salamar said. "You may answer directly."

Ishtar swallowed, looked around the dinner table, and felt beads of sweat rolling down his neck. He coughed, cleared his throat, then finally spoke as his tutors had taught him to speak. "I offer as evidence, oh wise one, the Greeks, the Romans, and your own Cholans. Are not they the greatest civilizations in all the history of the world? Do they not each attest to the fact that it takes many gods to rule the complex societies in which we live?"

For another ten minutes Ishtar gave a speech that impressed even his father. Drawing on his lessons in history, culture, politics, and religion, he wove together facts and ideas into an intricate argument. Everyone started eating again as Ishtar spoke. When Ishtar finished, the sheik nodded his head in understanding.

"I forgive your uncultured outburst as merely the uncontrolled emotions of a small boy," he said. "But you have made amends for your error as an educated man would, and I congratulate your father and your teachers for your fine education."

Ishtar's whole body relaxed, and he felt like he could breathe again.

"But," said the Sheik, "I disagree with your arguments, as well formed and stated as they were. Like many of your own Persian people, I am a follower of Zoroaster, who walked these very sands a thousand years ago. Zoroaster wrote clearly of the one true God who . . ."

Twenty minutes later the sheik finished his own arguments. Ishtar didn't agree at all, but by now his training in protocol and etiquette had returned to his thinking. "I bow to your wise and thoughtful arguments," he said.

The sheik smiled. "You are indeed well trained, for I suspect my comments have not changed your mind in the least." Ishtar wisely remained silent. "Let us end this discussion as friends, and as a friend I offer you this gift." He clapped twice and a servant placed a long, straight sack tied at both ends in Ishtar's hands. "A rare and magical invention from deep in China," the Sheik said, and everyone applauded his generosity.

Ishtar knew better than to open a gift in front of its giver, so just bowed again and thanked the sheik.

With his belly full of meat, cheese, bread, and olives, Ishtar headed back to his tent with Kazeem at his side. Most people were still awake, and many danced and sang around their fires. Once they reached the tent—which had been stitched together so well that it was hard to see where Kazeem's sword had sliced it open—Ishtar waited while his bodyguard inspected the interior. Kazeem was satisfied that it was safe, but Ishtar wasn't so sure. It was dark in there. What if Kazeem missed something? Even while he was thinking this, Kazeem had already grabbed a nearby torch and held it so Ishtar could see that no danger lurked inside.

"I am simply going to put my gift in the tent," Ishtar said. "Then you and I will stay up all night with the others dancing and singing."

"Yes, my young master," Kazeem said, but he didn't sound very sincere.

The body of the snake was gone, of course, but Ishtar was surprised that there wasn't even a hint of blood on the rugs and blankets. He tucked the gift into the space where the tent met the sand and turned to go. Then he saw his pillow and thought how good it would feel to lie down for just a moment. "Kazeem," he said through the flap, "I will rest a moment before we go out to play."

"Very good," Kazeem said.

It had been many hours since Ishtar's head had felt the cool silk and soft stuffing of the pillow, and the blankets that had felt scratchy the first night now seemed so plump and soft under his body that he coiled into a ball. He thought about the star they were expecting to guide them and wondered how such a tiny little light could lead this entire caravan on such a long journey. His eyes fell shut of their own free will, and within moments he was sound asleep.

"Kazeem!" Ishtar shouted, shading his eyes from the sun. "You didn't wake me!"

"Oh, but I tried, my young master!"

They were standing outside Ishtar's tent the next morning, Ishtar still framed by the door flap. He suspected that Kazeem hadn't really tried very hard, but had no proof.

"Very well. We shall go to my father's tent for breakfast."

On the way he saw that most of the caravan was sleeping, but some were over at the sheik's train talking and shopping. Uncle Jodhpur had brought a dozen wives on the trip, and Ishtar saw them buying perfumes and silks. It was a trader's caravan and carried jasmine and sugar, oil, amber, and peacock feathers.

Salamar greeted his son and told him what a fine performance he had given the evening before. The sheik had sent some leftover meat and cheese to Salamar's tent, and now all three sat and ate.

"Kazeem," Salamar said, "I believe this would be a good day to begin Ishtar's training."

Ishtar looked from his father to his bodyguard. "What training?"

"Kazeem is going to train you in the ways of the warrior," Salamar explained. "Persian men on horseback are the most fearsome and feared warriors in the world. It is one reason the Romans do not wish to war with us. As a prince, you must learn the ways of horse battle."

If there was one thing Ishtar feared more than camels it was horses. "B-but horses are so . . . *fast!*" he wailed.

"Which is why they make excellent mounts for battle," Salamar answered.

Ishtar knew there was no use arguing. If he'd learned one thing on this trip, it was that he had absolutely no say in what happened to him.

"Yes, Father," he said, slumping into a pout.

"But before your lessons begin," Salamar added, "you may open your gift from the sheik."

Ishtar sat up with a grin. "I forgot all about that!"

A few minutes later he was back at this tent, unrolling the gift. The package contained a patchwork of colorful silks sewn together, some sticks, and a ball of string.

"Most odd," Kazeem commented. "It looks like a tent too small to hold even a chicken."

Ishtar frowned as he turned it this way and that to see every side. Suddenly he gasped. "I know what this is!" he shouted.

"What?" asked Kazeem, but Ishtar didn't answer. Instead he ran out of the tent and to the outer edge of the caravan circle. "What is this thing?" Kazeem asked again.

Ishtar crossed the two sticks, tied them together, and attached the silk to the ends. When he finished he held up a diamond-shaped piece of silk stretched on a wooden frame. "There, you see?"

Kazeem shook his head slowly.

Ishtar sighed and wagged his head. "Oh, Kazeem, you are so old," he said. "You do not understand modern technology." Kazeem just shrugged helplessly. "It's a *kite!* I've heard about these from the traders who visit."

"What does it do?" Kazeem asked.

"It *flies!*"

Kazeem looked doubtful, but a few minutes later Ishtar had the kite in the air. Kazeem gasped as he watched the wind carry the kite high above the palm trees. "This is most amazing!"

After the wind died down and Ishtar retrieved his kite and stored it back in his tent, Kazeem introduced Ishtar to a horse twice his height. Ishtar learned how to sit in the saddle and steer the horse. After that it was an introduction to sword fighting, and after that an introduction to shooting a bow and arrow. "We'll work a little each day and by the time we return home you will be a great warrior," Kazeem said.

As the sun set, the camp came alive. Millet was passed about and the camels were loaded amidst their usual complaining. Ishtar watched the darkening sky, then shouted and pointed as the star appeared, and the caravan followed it away from the oasis and out into the empty desert. Ishtar was amazed at how much faster the camels moved in the cooler air of the night.

"I believe I will name him Musa," Ishtar said as he and Kazeem walked next to the camel train.

"Name who?"

"My camel, of course!"

"It is strange to name an animal," Kazeem said. "Animals are for work, not friendship."

"I think they can be for both," Ishtar answered, stroking his camel's beard. "He has been good to me. He never complains when I climb on him, and he no longer stinks."

Kazeem sighed. "Well, 'Musa' means 'companion,' so if you're going to name a camel I guess that's a very good name."

Ahead of them Ishtar saw that all the people were mounting their camels instead of walking, as if this were the heat of the afternoon.

"Snakes and scorpions live in the night," Kazeem explained. "On moonless nights like this it is best to ride." He lifted Ishtar up on Musa then climbed aboard his own camel. Ishtar saw three men on horseback emerge from the dark, then realized that the one in the lead was his father.

"Greetings, my son." Salamar turned his animal and fell into step alongside Ishtar. "And so we begin the difficult journey in the night."

"It is not so difficult from the back of a camel," Ishtar answered.

Salamar smiled, hesitated, then said, "Ishtar, there is something I must tell you." Ishtar thought his father looked worried, and that sent fear like a cobra snaking through his body.

"I must tell you, my son, a most dreadful secret."

Ishtar lived in a time and place where some people believe there are many gods. It was very common for people to have gods for everything—the sun, the moon, war, love, protection from snakes or famine. Often these gods were represented by little statues that people carried with them. People believed in these gods because they just didn't know any better.

That's why it's important for us to meet, and learn about, and understand the one true God for ourselves. We can't believe just because someone else does, we must come to know him as our own personal friend, and our own personal savior.

Jesus was born for just that reason. As both God and man, he knows what we're feeling, and what we need. The stories of him in Scripture give people a way to know him and love him, and have a friendship with him.

Enemies

Light the first two violet candles.

Ishtar tried to search the face of his father for a clue, but darkness kept it secret. Only the light of the special star lit Salamar, which gave him the appearance of a ghost.

"What is it, Father," Ishtar asked. "What is the secret?"

Salamar sighed. "I had hoped not to burden you, my son. But circumstances have forced it."

"*What* circumstances? Forced *what*?"

"Ishtar, the millet you almost ate for breakfast on the second day was not spoiled. It was poisoned."

"What!" Ishtar shouted.

"And the snake in your tent," Salamar continued, "did not crawl there on its own. There was no hole anywhere in the fabric."

Ishtar's mind was spinning so fast that he could fit no two thoughts together. "You mean," he said, "you mean, someone is trying to destroy the caravan?"

Salamar shook his head. "No, my son. Someone is trying to destroy *you*."

Once when he was young Ishtar had been running across the palace without looking and ran straight into a stone wall. His father's words now felt the same way.

"I-I—"

Salamar grasped his son's shoulder firmly. "You will be safe, Ishtar. Kazeem and Varta and I will protect you. But . . ."

"But *what*?"

"But we must take a few further precautions. Varta will keep a careful watch over your millet and water, and other food. And she has sharp eyes—sharper than Kazeem's. She will watch for any assassin that may approach in the night."

Ishtar didn't look too sure, so Salamar added, "Our culture may place women below men in importance Ishtar, but you will learn as you grow that there is little or nothing a man can do that a woman cannot."

Accepting this with a nod, Ishtar asked, "What else?"

"I am assigning these two soldiers to you." Ishtar looked at the men on the horses and thought they looked more dangerous than any assassin. "Mahmoud and Yazdan have been at my side for many years, and I trust them with my life. And yours."

There was silence for a moment until Salamar finally said, "Ishtar? What do you say?"

"Oh! Uh, I thank you for your loyal service to my father's house, and ask the gods to give you good health, and safety from the many . . . bad things . . . that evil and bad . . ."

Ishtar had no idea how to finish his sentence. Mahmoud laughed and smiled warmly. "You are most welcome, young prince."

Instantly Ishtar's opinion of the men changed. Not only did they seem kind, they had just saved him from an embarrassing social disaster.

Salamar leaned in close and lowered his voice. "I did not wish you to carry the burden of this knowledge, Ishtar, but we will soon celebrate the eleventh year of your birth and I think you are old enough to know the truth. And now that you know, you see how terribly important it is to follow all of our rules, and to do exactly what Kazeem and the others tell you."

Ishtar lowered his head. "Yes, Father."

And that's how Ishtar found himself flanked by Mahmoud on his left, Yazdan on his right, and Kazeem behind him. The camel-puller brought Varta's camel from the back of the file to the front, even as the caravan kept moving. He saw Varta sitting high in the saddle, her head constantly scanning the black night ahead.

"Can she even see anything?" Ishtar asked Kazeem.

"She has the vision of a horse," Kazeem answered. "As long as there's a star in the sky, a horse can see the road clearly, even when his rider sees only darkness."

Ishtar nodded, and began the long business of riding through the night.

And so it went for many weeks: rising from sleep just as the day ended to strike the camp and load the camels. Endless hours of walking the hard and rocky dirt in this empty land. Riding atop Musa on moonless nights. Taking lessons in horsemanship, swordsmanship, and archery in the cool of the morning, sleeping through the hot hours of the afternoon. Millet for breakfast, millet for lunch, millet for dinner, then camping at dawn to start again.

Through it all, Ishtar's mind would never let him forget that somewhere in the caravan lived an assassin appointed to kill him.

One morning during his lessons Ishtar was distracted by people shouting. Through the crowd he could see a man from another file, waist-deep in sand. The people formed a circle a good distance away from him, and a woman was screaming for someone to save her husband. The man sank lower and lower, until the sand almost reached his chin.

"Kazeem! You must go help!" Ishtar yelled.

"My duty is to you," Kazeem answered. "I cannot allow myself to be distracted from that duty, for such are the tricks of thieves and assassins."

Ishtar didn't understand. Finally a soldier on a horse threw the man a rope and pulled him to safety.

"What was *that*?" Ishtar asked.

"It was the devil sand," Kazeem answered. "It is invisible to the eye, but waits to swallow any who wander into its mouth."

Ishtar thought for a moment, then asked, "Would you have let the man die rather than leave my side?"

Kazeem looked at his ward slowly. "It is my sworn duty to protect you, Ishtar. I could not lower my diligence to save that man, nor could I to save Varta or even your father. My life is for you alone."

Ishtar thought about this for a very long time as he prepared for bed and fell asleep with those thoughts still in his mind.

One morning a swarm of locusts descended on the camp as Ishtar ate his dinner. One locust fell into Ishtar's millet, but he was so tired he didn't even care. He scooped up the millet, locust and all, and slurped it into his mouth. A bit crunchy, he thought, but not bad. From that moment on he began trying all sorts of things to improve the taste of the millet.

On a few occasions they stopped and set up camp near a caravan that was just starting their day. Each caravan was different, speaking different languages, wearing different clothes, believing in different gods.

On a particularly hot morning, after the camp was set up and most people were already asleep, Kazeem was putting the last stake in Ishtar's tent with his back to the desert. Ishtar could barely keep his eyes open he was so tired, but then something caught his eye—something bright red sitting on the sand about fifty camel paces away. Ishtar squinted, then jumped wide awake. It was a pomegranate! Suddenly visions of juicy pomegranate sliding across his tongue filled Ishtar's head. He started to run.

"Ishtar! Stop!" The command came from Kazeem but Ishtar was so tired it was several seconds before his brain understood the order and sent it to his feet. By then he'd gone three more strides and he suddenly felt the ground crumble and his feet grabbed by some strange force. Kazeem slid to a stop as he yelled for Mahmoud and Yazdan. "Ishtar! Do not move! Do not even wiggle your toes!"

Now Ishtar could feel the ground sucking at his ankles and he looked up, terrified.

"It is the devil sand," Kazeem yelled. "You will not sink if you do not move." The two other bodyguards arrived and threw a rope to Ishtar. "Tie it around your waist," Kazeem said. After Ishtar had done this, the bodyguards pulled slightly. "Now lift one foot very slowly and take a step, then lift the other one. But you must move slowly!"

By now Salamar had been summoned and came running up. "Do exactly as Kazeem says!" he yelled to Ishtar.

The muck was now halfway to Ishtar's knees. Ever so slowly, he pulled up with his right leg. At first his foot wouldn't move, but then it started to pull free. With a sucking sound, his right foot finally popped out of the sand. He took a step toward his father, and as he slowly pulled his left foot out, his right foot began to sink, but not as far as before. Working his way forward, with the rope around his waist giving him confidence, he eventually reached solid ground. He threw his arms around his father's waist, trembling.

"I'm sorry, Father," he said. "I just saw that fresh pomegranate and thought how good it would taste."

Kazeem had been staring at the fruit where it still lie, several rope-throws away. "What is a fresh pomegranate doing in the desert, in the middle of a bed of devil sand?" He and Salamar looked at each other, then looked across the huge circle of the camp with its hundreds of people settled for sleep.

"Would it have sucked me into the ground?" Ishtar asked his father.

"It is very unlikely. Most times a person sinks only to the knees and is stuck. More likely a passing snake or scorpion would have found you."

"But it is possible I could have been sucked under?"

Salamar nodded. "Yes, it is possible."

Several days later, Ishtar saw two men on horseback riding fast toward the caravan. He knew these were two of the guards who constantly scouted ahead for trouble. They reported to Rasad and Salamar, who then jumped on horses themselves and followed the men over the next hill. Ishtar was dying to know what was happening, but could only wait, slowly following the caravan up and down the barren hills.

Two hills later Salamar and Rasad returned.

"We are coming upon Zelzele," Salamar said, out of breath. "I have spoken to my friend Moez and he is alive, and all his family!" Ishtar thought he'd never seen his father so happy. "You shall meet them this very morning," Salamar said.

"Who is he?" Ishtar asked.

"A friend from the travels of my youth."

Ishtar was already thinking about the banquets and fine meals they'd be eating in Zelzele. Maybe there'd even be a swimming pool! Although, he did wonder about the name . . .

Over the crest of the next hill Ishtar saw the city of Zelzele rise from the sand. "That's *it*?" he shouted to Kazeem. He was expecting a city of stone and gold like Amaranth. Instead he saw a mish-mash of houses made of mud, all built into the rocks of a cliff, and all leaning this way and that. "Why would anyone want to live *there!*"

The caravan circled outside the town and everyone began their usual chores, but now with excitement in their work: a town—*any* town—was better than the desert!

A short time later Salamar returned on foot, walking with a man and a boy. Ishtar's guards started to go over to search them, but Salamar waved them away. *He's twice my father's age*, Ishtar thought of the man, who wore a long beard, a strange cap on his head, and a torn and dirty tunic. The boy, about Ishtar's age, was even worse, covered in dust and dirt, wearing a ragged and stained tunic. He was as skinny as a lizard and kept his eyes to the ground. Ishtar stared in disbelief.

"Ishtar," Salamar said, "this is my friend Moez, and his son Nami. They are guests in our tent."

Ishtar stared at the boy and could think of absolutely nothing kind to say except the standard greeting he'd been taught: "May the sheep on a thousand hilltops grace your father's flock, and may you find peace and joy among the tents of my father."

The boy looked up at Ishtar, scrunched up his nose, and said, "How come you talk so funny?"

Ishtar has felt what it's like to get sucked in by quicksand. Without someone there to save him, he might well have been consumed by the desert. Fortunately there is one by his side who will never leave him, not for anything. Kazeem has dedicated his life to protecting the young prince, and will never waver from that duty.

It's doubtful that you or I will ever stumble into quicksand, but there are many things in life that want to consume and destroy us. Things that are bad for us, but that look like fun, or emotions like hate and jealousy that pretend to make us feel good.

Fortunately there is One who stands beside us and will never leave us, not for anything. In fact he specifically said, "I will never leave you or forsake you." He's there every moment of our lives to help us, protect us, and guide us. Like Ishtar, we might start to get sucked in when we're not thinking, but if we realize our mistake and turn to him, Jesus will always be there.

Outpost

Light the first two violet candles.

Ishtar couldn't believe he'd just been insulted to his face. He was about to tell the dirty and ragged boy just who he was talking to when Nami's father held up his hand. "Forgive my son," he said with a bow. "We are a distant outpost, and we see mostly the rough and crude men of the trading caravans. We are not used to such refined people as yourselves."

"No offense is taken," Salamar said. "Correct, Ishtar?"

Ishtar wanted to say he took *great* offense, but knew that was not what his father expected. "No offense, Father," he said.

"Now, the matter of payment for use of your well," Salamar continued to Moez. "I know you are a shrewd trader, and hard negotiator for your village. But I want you to know that I am too, and we will pay not one grain more than fifteen sacks for the right to water our entire caravan."

"Fifteen sacks!" Ishtar yelled. "But, Father, that is—" He stopped talking when his father shot him a sharp look. "That is . . . very shrewd of you . . ." Ishtar finished.

"And we shall need enough salt for our animals for a month. Five more sacks of grain."

Moez scratched his beard as if considering the offer. "Are you sure I cannot bargain you out of a few more sacks?" Salamar shook his head. Moez sighed, then said, "Agreed!"

At that moment Varta arrived with her bag of millet. While everyone was paying attention to her Ishtar whispered to Salamar. "Father! Fifteen sacks is three times more—" Salamar held up his hand and Ishtar knew to be quiet.

"Excuse the interruption," Varta said, "but Ishtar must have his dinner."

"Dinner?" Nami said. "But the sun just came up! It is time for breaking fast."

“Our days are backwards,” Salamar explained. “We travel at night and sleep in the day.”

Varta poured Ishtar’s millet. Having no locust handy to put in the slop, Ishtar held his nose and drank it down. Moez and Nami both stared at the empty cup.

“Perhaps Nami and his father would like to share in your dinner,” Salamar said to Ishtar.

“I would not wish that upon my nastiest enemy,” Ishtar said. But Varta poured another cupful and handed it to Nami. Nami gulped it down with great pleasure, as did Moez a moment later.

“I have not had such a wonderful breakfast in many days,” Nami said, wiping his mouth.

“You think that was *wonderful*?” Ishtar gasped.

Salamar decided it was time to change the subject. “Moez, let us talk in the comfort of my tent.”

“Excellent,” Moez said. Then to his son, “Nami, show Ishtar around Zelzele.”

“Yes, Father,” Nami answered.

Ishtar followed Nami across the camp and into the town, with Kazeem close behind, even though it was his turn to rest. Zelzele was a town of about two hundred houses, all built on the side of a hill that overlooked the desert for many miles in every direction. Many of the buildings were connected, so that if you wanted to get to a house in the middle, you’d have to go through five or six other houses to get there. The thick mud walls leaned precariously under roofs formed by wooden boards covered with palm branches.

Most of the narrow streets were more like paths, and had a roof over them to provide shade from the harsh sun. Everywhere they went there were stairs going this way and that, some crumbling to rubble.

I can’t wait to get away from this dry, dirty place, Ishtar thought.

“Would you like to be my friend?”

Nami’s question startled Ishtar. “Uh, of course,” he said, though he wasn’t really sure. He’d never in his life had a friend, except Kazeem. And his cousins. *But they don’t count because they’re family*, Ishtar thought.

“I’ll show you the whole city!” Nami said, and Ishtar thought he seemed awfully excited. They walked up and down the steep and narrow streets.

“Why is your town called *Zelzele*?” The word meant “earthquake” and Ishtar couldn’t figure out why anyone would name a town that.

Nami looked at Ishtar as if he'd just claimed to be a camel. "Do you not see?" he asked.

Ishtar finally realized and felt as dumb as a brick. "This town was *destroyed* by an earthquake!"

Nami nodded.

"But what was its name before that?"

"No one knows," Nami answered. "It fell many centuries ago. Then my father's father's grandfather settled here and gave it its new name. But back then water flowed freely and there was a great oasis here."

"Well, why not move to someplace better?" Ishtar asked.

Nami shrugged. "It is home."

Suddenly Nami stopped and spun toward Ishtar. "Home! It is the noon hour! You must come to my home for the midday meal," he said.

Nami led them up a particularly twisted street barely wide enough for Kazeem's broad shoulders, then they ducked down into a dark hole in the wall. Inside, when his eyes finally adjusted, Ishtar saw that the hole was Nami's home—a single room with a fire pit in the middle and bed sacks around the outside. The only light in the room filtered through the palm branches of the roof. There were several children playing with sticks and rocks and one little rag doll.

"These are my three little sisters and two little brothers," Nami said of the children. "And this is my mother," he added, pointing to a woman stirring the fire. "Mother, this is my new friend Ishtar. He is a prince of all Persia!"

Nami's mother raised her eyebrows in surprise and said, "Welcome to our home, young prince. Please, stay and take your noon meal with us."

"I would be most honored," Ishtar said. His stomach had been protesting the lack of food ever since . . . well, ever since they left the first oasis weeks ago he realized. It would be good to have a real meal. Nami seemed very proud to give his new friend a tour of the one-room house while his mother cooked, though Ishtar didn't think the place was fit for even Musa to sleep. "This is my bed," Nami said, pointing to one of the flat bags filled with straw. "And this is my pet giraffe," he added, holding up a piece of cloth that had been knotted into something resembling the animal. "His name is Musa."

"Musa is the name of my camel!" Ishtar said, and Nami laughed.

"My father says that only the Romans name their animals."

Ishtar looked at Kazeem as he answered Nami. "That's what some people have told me, too."

Nami's mother called them to eat and they all sat around the little cooking fire, except for Kazeem who stood by the door. Nami's mother sat with her back to Kazeem, and Ishtar sat looking at her from across the fire pit. The other children filled in around them.

Ishtar looked at the meal and thought, this is ridiculous! On the pan over the fire were nine tiny, lifeless pieces of flatbread and three even smaller pieces of meat.

"The meat is for our guests," Nami's mother said. Then she prayed to the gods a blessing over the food, and Ishtar thought that if they were really gods they'd be able to multiply the food and help his starving friends. But when she was done, there remained only the pitifully small portions on the grill. Nami's brothers and sisters each snatched their piece of bread and shoved it in their mouths. In moments it was gone, barely a single bite.

"I had a most wonderful cup of millet this morning," Nami said, "and am still full." He handed his piece of bread to his mother.

"And I require no food," Kazeem said from where he stood.

Nami's mother took those two pieces of bread, tore them in two, and gave them to the four youngest children. "I am not so hungry myself," she said, giving half her piece of bread to the fifth child.

All that was left on the flat cooking pan were the three pieces of meat and the one piece of bread. Ishtar's stomach was still screaming from hunger, but his heart was hurting even more. The faces of the five small children were all looking at him, and he knew they were starving.

"I . . . I have eaten far too much on this journey," he said. "Please, take . . ." At that moment he saw Kazeem shaking his head quickly with wide-open eyes. He was mouthing the words, "No! You must eat!"

Ishtar stopped in mid-sentence, then realized there must be some rule of etiquette involved. He didn't know which one, but knew better than to violate it. "Uh, please, take my most humble thanks for this wonderful meal," he said, and Kazeem nodded and smiled.

Then, feeling terribly guilty, and with his heart still hurting as the hungry children watched, he ate all of the meat and bread, making sure to look as if it were the finest banquet he'd ever attended.

Ishtar could still see the faces of the starving children in his mind's eye as he, Nami, and Kazeem walked back to the caravan. He saw that about half the camels had been watered and half the water bags filled from the only well in the city, and wondered what was taking so long.

"Father," Ishtar called as they entered Salamar's tent, "may I speak with you?"

Salamar excused himself from Moez and followed Ishtar to the other end of the tent. "Father, I know now why you over-paid for the water," Ishtar whispered. "But it is not enough! We must give Moez many more bags of grain!"

Salamar smiled. "Your heart is good and kind," he said, "but we cannot. I paid Moez as much as I thought we could and still make it seem a fee for the water and salt. Any more would be seen as charity, and that would be an insult."

"But his children are *starving!*"

"Yes, I know. But twenty sacks of grain will give them good nourishment for many months." He stopped and looked at Ishtar for several moments, waiting to see if his son would see his plan, then added, "Many months—until we travel through here on our way home, and need water and salt again."

Ishtar smiled. "I see my father is more devious than I knew."

"Perhaps you will someday learn that your father knows a great deal more than you think he does."

Ignoring that remark, Ishtar spoken even softer. "Father, I know that the eleventh year of my birth is soon to pass, and I know that, even on a caravan in the middle of the desert, you would not let it pass without a celebration."

"And so," Salamar answered, "what thought is filling your head?"

Ishtar cleared his throat. "I would like to ask you for a very special birthday gift this year," he said.

And his next words surprised even Salamar.

Compassion is a hard thing to learn. It means genuinely caring for someone else who is hurt or has a need. Compassion requires us to be more concerned for the other person than we are for our own needs and desires.

It requires us to let go of our selfishness.

The only life Ishtar has ever known has been the life of rich foods, royal palaces, and servants. But when faced with people in terrible hunger, he finally realizes that he's had it easy, while other people suffer. And it hurts him so much that he wants to change.

He wants to give up his selfishness.

Can we do that? Can we stop worrying about ourselves, and put the needs of others ahead of our own?

Can we learn . . . compassion?

Birthday Surprise

Light the first two violet candles.

Salamar took a deep breath. "And what is this special birthday gift you would like?"

Ishtar looked his father in the eyes. "I know that you will have some packages of baklava and other fine treats for my birth celebration. For my birthday, I wish to have those now, to give to the children in Zelzele. They have nothing, when I have everything. I will never eat a piece of baklava again without feeling guilty."

Salamar smiled at his son. "You have learned much already on this journey. And I shall grant your birthday wish." He clapped twice and gave orders for the treats to be unpacked and given to Ishtar.

Meanwhile, Ishtar ran to find Varta who had just finished cooking the day's allotment of millet. Grabbing the bag without stopping, Ishtar yelled, "Thank you, Varta!" The old woman looked up in shock as she saw her work running away. He then called to Nami and together they raced back to his new friend's house, with Kazeem in pursuit.

The children were lying on their beds. They weren't asleep, but they weren't moving either. Ishtar turned to Nami's mother and said, "A most kind act requires a most generous show of thanks. With this millet, and these pastries, I pay my debt of thanks to you for the wonderful noon meal."

Nami's mother started to protest, then accepted Ishtar's kindness with a nod. "Children! Our friend Ishtar has brought food. Come and eat."

The children all scrambled to the center of the room where their mother poured cups of millet. After that, Ishtar and Nami passed out pieces of baklava, gaz, and other treats. The childrens' faces lit up with the sweet taste of the pastries. "That is the best birthday present I could ever have," Ishtar said under his breath.

"What was that?" Nami's mother asked.

"Oh, nothing," Ishtar answered.

Late that afternoon the caravan had finally been watered. Half the people had been sleeping and now awoke to prepare for travel. "Ten thousand pardons," Moez said to Salamar with a bow. "Our well water gets lower every day, but we do not have the skill or the strength to dig it any deeper. That is why we use nothing for bathing—we must save as much as we can to sell to passing caravans."

"Father! We should dig it deeper for them!" Ishtar said. "Surely we have men who know how to do this thing."

"Alas," Salamar answered, "it is not in our ability to do so. We are slaves to the star, and must follow it as long as it leads."

Ishtar was sad, and continued to be sad as the tents were packed and the camels loaded. The sun set as they ate their evening millet. Ishtar thought it tasted much better than before, even without locusts. They said goodbye to Moez, Nami, and all their friends.

As the last of the light faded and all the camels were tied together, Salamar rode back along the files to Ishtar, who sat waiting on Musa.

"Ishtar!" his father called, and for a moment he thought he was in trouble. "Do you see the star? Sometimes it appears to you when others cannot find it."

Ishtar scanned the sky, focusing in on the constellation of Sagr. Finally he said, "No, it is not there. I do not see it anywhere."

Salamar sighed, then thought for several moments. Suddenly a thought struck Ishtar and he sat straight up in the saddle. "I know!" he yelled. "The star is telling us to stay here and help Moez with his well!"

Another sigh. "I believe you have interpreted this sign correctly. Or rather, this *lack* of a sign. We shall stay."

Ishtar cheered and the order was given to dismount and set up the tents again. Although it made extra work, no one complained about the opportunity for a good night's rest.

The next morning Salamar organized a work crew to dig the well deeper. Ishtar watched as a man would climb over the rock wall of the well and be lowered to the bottom. Nami told him its depth was greater than the height of five houses. At the bottom of the well the man would shovel mud into a bucket, which was then hauled up and emptied. Any one man could only work a short time because of the foul air at the bottom of the well, so they'd pull him up, then another man would go down.

"When we have dug the hole into the water about waist high," the supervisor explained, "we will line it with rocks."

Ishtar and Nami explored the city all afternoon, occasionally checking on the progress of the well. Nami showed him the salt pits, where water seeping up through the ground mixes with minerals to form salt. Ishtar watched as men splashed the heavy brine back and forth so the water would evaporate. Once dried, other men would pound the chunks of salt with wooden mallets to crush it, then it would be served as table salt for people, or molded into long pillars for the animals.

Ishtar heard one man from his caravan bargaining with one of the salt sellers.

"Please, sir," the seller was saying, "I ask only a fair price, to feed my children."

"If you do not want to sell me salt I shall just wait until the next town," the buyer said.

The seller was a small man, and weak from hunger. "But what you offer is unreasonable. You are taking advantage of the hunger of my family."

"Take my offer now or I shall leave," the buyer said, holding out what looked to Ishtar like a spoonful of grain in a bag. Without another word the seller took the grain and handed the man a large cake of salt.

By mid-afternoon the well had been dug deep enough that the water was waist high on the workers.

"Magnificent!" shouted Moez. "I shall find some way to repay your for your kindness, but for now please accept the gratitude of the entire village."

"I am paid by the knowledge that you and your kinfolk will live and be healthy," Salamar said.

As the sun began to set, no one knew if the star would again appear in the sky. Most everyone had tried to sleep for a short time, so they'd be prepared to travel if it did. Now they waited and ate their dinner in circles around small cooking fires. Ishtar walked the whole camp with Nami. As he passed one group he heard the man who bought the salt telling his story.

"The man was a beast—a head taller than myself! But I looked him in the eye and said, 'My offer is generous, and more than I would have to pay anywhere else. Fight me if you wish, but I have righteousness on my side!' The man drew his sword and threatened to steal all I had, but I stood my ground and soon he backed down."

The people listening laughed and applauded. By now Ishtar considered all of Zelzele his friends, and could not stand to hear them talked about in lies. But what could he do? He was just a boy. With his anger building, he marched into the center of the ring and yelled, "Liar!"

Everyone stopped talking and looked at Ishtar. Nami's mouth had dropped open. "I was there when you made your bargain, and I know you cheated a starving man out of his fair wages. You have made the *poz dadan*, and I turn my back on you!" Then he spun around, arms crossed, and hung his head in shame for the man.

The others around the circle stared first at Ishtar, then at the man, then back again. Even if he had not been a prince of Persia, something in Ishtar's words, or something they knew of the other man, convinced them that Ishtar told the truth. Slowly, one by one, all who sat around the fire stood and turned their backs to the salt buyer, and hung their heads.

Anyone else would have been shamed into confessing their sin and making amends, but the man just stormed off, flashing at Ishtar a look of hate.

By now the sun had set, and Ishtar turned his gaze to the sky without thinking. "The star!" he shouted. "I see the star!" His father heard and came running over. He verified Ishtar's sighting, then ordered the camels loaded.

The animals complained loudly as they were loaded, and in the commotion Ishtar almost forgot about Nami. "I shall miss you!" he said to his friend.

"And I you."

Ishtar grasped Nami's forearm in the traditional greeting. "If the gods will allow, I shall return this way in a few months," he said. Then a thought flew into his head and he added, "Wait here!" He ran to Musa, who had already been loaded, and asked Kazeem to help him find his spare tunic. Then he ran back to Nami and held it out for the boy. "I wish you to have this as my gift of friendship."

Nami gaped at the relatively clean and whole tunic. "I . . . I am honored!" he said.

"Then let this be a promise between us, that we shall be friends for the rest of our lives."

Ishtar climbed up on Musa—no longer needing Kazeem to lift him—the two bells rang, and the caravan jerked forward into its slow and steady pace, with Kazeem walking behind Ishtar, and the two guards riding to either side. Nami kept waving from the edge of the village until darkness and the distance hid him from view, and Ishtar wondered what other surprising things lay in his path.

Jesus came to earth as almighty, all-powerful God, yet he didn't find it necessary to boast and brag about his power. But we mere humans often feel the need to boast and brag about our small and insignificant accomplishments.

Often we do that because we feel like we're not very good, like other people are better than we are, and we need to prove ourselves.

That's how the man in Ishtar's camp was. He thought he could impress everyone by making himself seem big and important. It didn't work.

Usually it doesn't work for us, either. And the truth is we don't *need* to boast, for the same reason Jesus didn't: we're already big and important. Our God thinks we're his most important creation, and he loves us enough to sacrifice himself for us.

Jesus didn't need to boast. Neither do we. God will do all the boasting about us that needs to be done.

> This is what the LORD says: "Let not the wise man boast of his wisdom or the strong man boast of his strength or the rich man boast of his riches, but let him who boasts boast about this: that he understands and knows me, that I am the LORD, who exercises kindness, justice and righteousness on earth, for in these I delight," declares the LORD. JEREMIAH 9:23–24

Attack

Light the first two violet candles.

Two days later the caravan crossed another trade route, and now they passed other sleeping caravans every few nights. Many times as they stopped in the morning they would trade goods, stories, and news with others nearby. Even Salamar got excited one morning when he found an old scroll among the items a caravan was selling. "Ishtar! Look at this! A scroll of the Torah written in old Umbrian!"

"Oh, great," Ishtar said with no enthusiasm.

"And you keep calling this a dead language! Here," Salamar said, pointing to a line in the middle of the scroll, "read this."

Ishtar sighed, but obeyed. "Uh, it says, 'But you, Bethlehem . . .' what's this word?"

Salamar leaned in and studied the scroll. "Ephrathah," he said.

"'But you, Bethlehem Ephrathah, though you are small among the, uh, clans of Judah, out of you will come for me one who will be ruler over Israel, whose, um, origins are from of old, from ancient times.'"

"Do you know what that means?" Salamar asked. Ishtar shook his head. "It is one of the pieces of evidence your uncles and I used in interpreting the appearance of the star. This scripture *could* be referring to the new king."

"Then why don't we just go to this Bethlehem place?"

Salamar laughed. "We follow the star, Ishtar, only the star."

Salamar bartered for the scroll, saying his friend Nathan would find it fascinating. A perfect gift.

Just before the sky turned pink with daylight one morning, Ishtar rode atop Musa through an area of low hills. It had been a particularly long night, and he had a hard time staying awake. He strained to open his eyelids, only to have them snap shut again a moment later. Finally he gave up, laid his head on Musa's front hump, and was instantly asleep.

Ishtar jerked awake and grabbed on tightly as Musa made a frightful noise and started bucking wildly as if he'd gone mad. A moment later Ishtar was flying through the air, head-over-heels. He saw the rocky ground coming toward him and tried to cover his head as he screamed.

Instead of hitting the rocks, Ishtar felt himself land in something soft, and something that broke his fall. He opened his eyes to see that he was in the arms of a frightened Kazeem.

"What happened?" Ishtar yelled as the two guards took up positions on either side, watching out into the desert.

"I do not know," Kazeem said. "Probably a snake."

"But we have seen many snakes, and Musa just ignores them."

Kazeem didn't answer, and instead set Ishtar down and walked over to Musa, who was now lying on his side, breathing hard. In the darkness, Kazeem ran his hands over the animal, checking for injuries. When he reached Musa's right front shoulder he stopped and held up his hand. Even in the light of the stars, Ishtar could see it was covered in blood.

"What happened!" Ishtar gasped.

Again Kazeem didn't answer, and instead began searching the ground. He bent to pick something up, and a moment later showed Ishtar an arrow.

At that moment Rasad and Ishtar's father rode up to see what the disturbance was about. Kazeem quickly explained what had happened.

Ishtar was still trying to figure it out. "Why would someone want to shoot Musa with an arrow?" he said.

Salamar once again shot Kazeem a look, but this time Ishtar saw it. "What?" he said. "What is it you're hiding from me?"

"Ishtar," his father said softly, "it is unlikely the arrow was intended for Musa."

Ishtar didn't understand for several seconds, but then it hit him. "Someone was trying to shoot *me*?"

"It is possible," Salamar said, stretching his neck to look around in the growing light, though he knew the shooter would be long gone.

"Morning is upon us," Rasad said. "We shall make camp here." Then he looked at Musa and added, "This animal is injured. We shall leave it behind." Then Rasad rode off to find out who was shooting arrows at his caravan.

"Leave Musa!" Ishtar yelled. "We cannot leave Musa! He is my friend!"

Salamar sighed. "Mus . . . *this animal* is injured," he said. "It will be unable to walk and will slow us down. We cannot allow that."

"No!" Ishtar cried. "We cannot leave him!"

Salamar looked at his son with sad eyes. "We shall talk of this later," he said. "But now we have a more urgent matter." He quickly gave orders to Kazeem to do some investigation while Mahmoud and Yazdan watched over Ishtar. As the caravan began setting up the tents Kazeem brought an old man who had been gathering dried camel dung in the desert to burn.

"This is Faraj," Kazeem introduced the man. "He is from three files back, and has news."

"What is it you know?" Salamar asked the man.

Faraj drew a deep breath, obviously nervous to be talking to the chief Magi himself. "A few minutes before we stopped," he said, "I saw a man come from somewhere behind us, carrying a bow. He went off to the right of the caravan, but then was hidden by the hills."

The old man coughed, and Ishtar thought he should have Varta make him a cup of hot tea.

"Can you describe the man?" Salamar asked.

Faraj shrugged. "He was a little taller than me, wearing a dirty white tunic and blue trousers."

Ishtar, Kazeem, and Salamar all scanned the hundreds of men setting up tents and unloading camels. "That describes just about every man in the caravan," Kazeem said.

"It is the best I can do. I did not see his face."

Salamar thanked the old man.

"I know who did this," Ishtar said, anger in his voice.

"Who?" his father asked. "And how could you know?"

"I do not know his name, but I know his face. He is in the file with the dark camel, and has a scar on his chin. I caught him making the *poz dadan* and he was very angry."

"I know this man," Kazeem said. "I shall question him."

When Kazeem had gone, Ishtar turned to his father. "What about Musa?"

Salamar thought for a moment. "I will send a camel-puller known as The Healer who is an expert at treating the animals. If he says the animal can travel, all is well. But if he says it must be left behind, it will be so."

Kazeem came back and reported the scarred man had not left his file all morning, but Ishtar didn't believe it. Salamar returned to his tent while The Healer finished his work. "The arrow went straight through his shoulder, which is good," the healer said to Ishtar. "But it nicked a bone on the way, which is bad. The animal will be in great pain and will walk very slowly. Eventually it will get infected and then he will not be able to walk at all."

"Please!" Ishtar said. "There must be something you can do!"

"If we were not in the middle of the desert, perhaps. But look for yourself—do you see any trees or bushes, any herbs growing or flowers blooming?"

"If there were, what would we look for?" Ishtar asked.

The camel-puller shrugged. "By far the best would be an ointment of myrrh, but we are many weeks ride from any myrrh trees."

Ishtar opened his mouth to say something, but then remembered his father's words and said only, "I will ask my father if he knows where we might obtain some." He walked away from the man, but as soon as he was out of sight he ran the rest of the way to his father's tent, forcing Yazdan to run to keep up. Ishtar found his father already in his bed, sound asleep, and snoring.

"Father, Father!" he yelled as he shook Salamar. "I have a most urgent favor to ask of you."

"Wha . . . What is it!" Salamar yelled, grumbling awake.

"I must ask of you a most urgent favor!" Ishtar said again.

Salamar blinked rapidly, trying to wake his brain.

"I know that the three special gifts we carry are for the child king," Ishtar said slowly, stitching his thoughts together with care. "But I also know that my father would not embark on such a journey as this without some *extra* amount of gifts, in case some were lost or stolen."

"Yes, and so?" Salamar said, fully awake now.

"And so, I was wondering if I could have just a small amount of myrrh. The camel-puller says it would help Musa to heal."

Salamar let out his all-too-familiar sigh, a sigh that Ishtar had come to hate. "We cannot waste such precious cargo on a mere animal . . ."

"Musa," Ishtar said.

"What?"

"I said, Musa. His name is Musa."

"But he is only an . . ."

"Please don't call him an animal, Father. Please just say his name."

"Very well," Salamar gave in. "We cannot waste such precious cargo on . . . Mu . . . Musa."

"On *who*?" Ishtar asked.

"I said it . . . on the camel Musa."

"What did you call him?"

Salamar was exasperated now. "Musa!" he almost shouted.

"Good," Ishtar said, crossing his arms and smiling. "You have said his name three times, and by tradition he is now your friend and you must help him."

"There is no such tradition!" Salamar roared.

"It is *my* tradition," Ishtar answered. "I just made it up."

Salamar sputtered and spat for a moment, stopped for another moment, then burst out laughing.

"Very well," he said. "I suppose we can spare a small amount." He gave the order, and a few minutes later Ishtar was running back to his own tent.

"My father had a bit of myrrh packed for just such an event," he told The Healer, who took the spice.

With a flat stick, The Healer mixed it with some honey. "You must be very careful not to smell the fumes of the medicine. It will give you instantly a very bad headache."

"I have smelled myrrh many times. It is a most pleasing incense."

"You speak of myrrh which has been processed. This is raw myrrh sap straight from the tree." Ishtar watched as The Healer spread the myrrh on the bandage, then wrapped the bandage on the wound. "You must do this twice each day," he said.

"You want *me* to change the bandage?"

"Yes, of course," The Healer answered. "I have my own camels to tend to. Besides, he is *your* friend."

Ishtar thanked The Healer, then Kazeem said it was time for both Musa and Ishtar to rest. Ishtar was exhausted, but thoughts of how close the arrow had come, and worries about Musa, kept him awake until well past noon.

That night after breakfast the star appeared and everyone broke camp and loaded the camels. Musa was still lying on the ground, and Ishtar knew what that meant. "Musa! You must get up!" he whispered to the camel, pulling on his reins. Musa just looked at him sadly and remained on the ground.

Ishtar looked up to see his father and the *karvan-salar* walking toward him. "Quick Musa! You must stand up now!" But tug as he might, the camel just lay on his side, his head resting on the ground.

Rasad walked up, looked at Musa for a moment, said, "Very well, then, it is decided," then turned and walked away.

Ishtar knows his father well. He knew his father wouldn't let his birthday pass without bringing along something with which to celebrate, he knew his father would bring extra myrrh just in case some got lost or stolen, and he knew just how to convince his father to care about Musa.

Ishtar knows his father very, very well.

Shouldn't we know our *heavenly* Father just as well? Shouldn't we know what he's thinking even without asking? Shouldn't we understand what pleases him, and hurts him, and causes him to care about the things we care about?

Ishtar knows his father well because he's spent his entire life watching and listening to and talking with him.

How can we can get to know our heavenly Father that well?

The Law

Light the first two violet candles.

Ishtar watched Rasad walk away, having condemned Musa to be left behind. *"No!"* he yelled, but Rasad kept walking. "This is ridiculous!" Then he turned to Salamar. "Father! Musa saved my life!"

"Yes, he did," Salamar answered. "And this is the price he must pay for his bravery. He trades his life for yours, such as any good friend would do." Ishtar began to cry and Salamar pulled him close. "I am sorry, but we cannot endanger the entire caravan for one injured camel."

Ishtar looked at Musa through blurry eyes, thinking of the many hours he'd spent with the camel. Then, as if he was remembering too, Musa suddenly pulled his legs under him and stood up.

"He's standing! Father! He's standing!"

"So I see," said Salamar.

Rasad heard the commotion and came walking back. "You see!" Ishtar shouted. "He is feeling much better and can walk now."

Rasad looked the camel up and down, then turned to Ishtar. "He is still injured, and will still slow us down. He must be left behind." With that, Rasad turned and walked away once more.

All the anger and frustration Ishtar felt exploded from inside him. "Why are you so mean!" he screamed.

Rasad turned slowly, came back to Ishtar, and got down on one knee. "I am not mean," he said. "I only follow the law and rules that govern our lives. The law of the one true God, and the rules of survival. I am sorry for your camel, but he must be sacrificed for the good of all."

"There are many gods, not one," Ishtar said, "and this is just a rule you made up."

"I am a Jew and I live under one God, and he is a god of laws and rules—all meant to keep our feet on a safe path."

Salamar cleared his throat. "*Karvan-salar*, the operation of the caravan is most assuredly your responsibility, and I would not try to oppose your authority. But is there not room in your knowledge of camels to allow for the possibility that Musa might be able to keep up with us?"

Rasad looked at the camel in disgust, then to the camel healer. "What say you?" he asked.

The Healer studied Musa for several moments, then said, "He is much recovered, and much stronger. He may perhaps be able to walk. But he cannot carry a load."

"Very well," Rasad said with a sigh. "You may bring him along. But do not ride him, and do not even put a saddle on his back."

"No sir, I will not!" Ishtar said, now grinning.

Salamar smiled at his son, then the three men went back to their duties. Kazeem loaded Musa's saddle on top of the load of another camel and the caravan wobbled into motion. The moon was bright and it was easy to see, so Ishtar walked for many hours. Eventually Kazeem brought him a horse to ride. "We will now begin training at night as well," he said. "You are becoming a good horseman, and a good archer. It is time for you to learn the Parthian Shot."

"What is *that*?" Ishtar asked.

Kazeem sighed and shook his head. "With all your lessons, do they not teach you the most important things in life?" he said. Ishtar didn't answer, so Kazeem explained. "The Parthian Shot is a special technique that only we Persians know. It allows us to shoot backwards, *behind* our horse, in the midst of battle."

"How will I see on nights there is no moon?" Ishtar protested.

"You do not need to see. The horse will see for you."

Twice each day Ishtar changed the bandage on Musa, applying new ointment. On the third day it was becoming routine, and Ishtar got a bit lazy. As he spread the ointment on the bandage he yawned and sucked in a deep breath of the toxic fumes. Instantly his head felt like it was splitting open. He held his head tightly and began screaming.

"You are not injured," the camel healer said after examining Ishtar. "But your head will hurt for a few hours."

By the fifth night Musa was strong enough to carry a saddle, and on the seventh Ishtar started riding him again. It was then that Ishtar thought up a plan.

"Father, I know how to catch the assassin!"

The day was young, and Salamar was in his tent reading some scrolls, but now looked at his son with curiosity. Kazeem had questioned everyone in the caravan but had no idea who was behind the attacks on the prince.

Salamar laid down his scrolls. "I'm listening."

Ishtar told him the plan, and Salamar liked it, then Kazeem liked it, and even Rasad said he'd go along with it.

The next day was the eleventh anniversary of Ishtar's birth. In honor of that, Salamar cancelled Ishtar's lessons and declared it a day of feasting: whatever foods could be gathered would be prepared for the occasion. "But no millet!" Ishtar said.

Salamar laughed. "No millet," he repeated.

Everyone enjoyed the celebration, held during the cool of the morning since their days were still backward. Salamar commanded that the entire caravan gather together, and there was singing and dancing and eating. Salamar even brought out a piece of baklava he'd held back just for Ishtar. During it all Kazeem, Varta, Mahmoud and Yazdan kept a careful watch to make sure there were no attempts on Ishtar's life. They were very obvious and conspicuous about protecting Ishtar so that no one in the camp could possibly miss them.

As the sun edged toward the top of the sky people began to get sleepy—it was time for bed. With a final cheer for Ishtar, Salamar thanked the people and then dismissed them to sleep through the day.

Immediately, Ishtar, Kazeem, Varta and the two soldiers rushed back to Ishtar's tent. While the others waited outside, Kazeem held his breath, held his nose, and entered through the flap. A few moments later he came back out, holding in his hand a black creature. "A fat-tail scorpion," Kazeem said. "Most deadly. Its poison kills in minutes. It was hiding between your bed blankets," Kazeem said with a frown, "and I do not believe he chose to hide there on his own."

None of the other five were at all surprised. "Then you must hurry," Ishtar said.

Kazeem nodded, handed the scorpion to Mahmoud, then leaving Ishtar in the care of the others he headed out across the camp. While he was gone, Salamar arrived.

"Well?" he said, "What is the news?"

In answer, Mahmoud held out the scorpion. Salamar simply pursed his lips and nodded. They all waited in silence, but only a few minutes later Kazeem returned, followed by Faraj, the old man who had seen the man who shot an arrow at Ishtar. Faraj walked bent over, stumbled twice, and held his head in obvious pain.

"What is this?" Salamar asked. "A man in great pain?"

Faraj looked up at Salamar. "A most devilish pain in my head, oh noble one. Kazeem said you might have a cure for me."

Salamar and Ishtar both looked at the man with disgust. "I most certainly have a cure for the pain in your head," Salamar said, drawing his sword, "but I shall leave it to the gods to decide your fate."

Faraj looked up again, confused, then he saw the sword. "M-my master! What have I done to displease you!"

Salamar didn't answer. Instead, Mahmoud simply held up the scorpion for the old man to see. Faraj started to tremble, then slumped to the ground. At that moment Rasad rode up on his horse.

"What news is there?" he yelled, as the horse slid to a stop. "Did Ishtar's plan work?"

"Indeed it did," said Salamar. Then he pulled back the flap of Ishtar's tent and in moments the air was filled with the scent of myrrh. "You see, Faraj, we set out several pots of unprocessed myrrh in Ishtar's tent. It was the fumes from those pots that gave you the terrible pain in the head—as you hid *this* in Ishtar's bed!" Salamar took the scorpion and held it right in the face of Faraj. The old man jumped back.

Kazeem stepped in. "You were the only one in camp with a pain in the head after the celebration," he said. "It must have been you who placed the scorpion there."

"And shot Musa with the arrow!" Ishtar added.

"And lured Ishtar into the devil sand with the pomegranate," Varta said.

"And placed the snake in his tent," added Kazeem.

"And poisoned his millet," Salamar said slowly, once again holding the scorpion in front of the old man's face. Then he whispered, "There is no escape now."

In a moment the look on the old man's face changed. No longer kindly and gentle, he set his jaw, clenched his lips, and narrowed his eyes. "What I did, I did for my people," he spat. "This false prince must die, and all his family with him!"

Salamar was stunned. "What insult have we inflicted on you that you would attempt to kill my son?"

Faraj looked at them all with even more contempt. "My name is not Faraj, it is Fajad, and I come from the people of the Seleucids, whom you Persians conquered and destroyed without mercy!"

Salamar stood and shook his head slowly. "That was three centuries ago," he said, "and history makes villains of both sides. Why do you fill your heart with hatred for something that happened long before you were born?"

"The gods demand revenge," Fajad answered, "no matter how long it takes."

"Then your gods are weak and cowardly," Salamar said, "for only a coward would block reconciliation from his heart."

Rasad ordered two soldiers to bind the elderly assassin, then led him away. "We are almost to Seleucia," he said, "and within their territory. We will turn him over to authorities there."

"Isn't that the home of his own people?" Ishtar said. "Will they not just let him go?"

"The city still carries the name," Salamar answered, "but the people have carried no ill will toward Parthia for two centuries."

"What will they do to him?"

Salamar put his arm around Ishtar's shoulders. "He will be punished as their law demands. I do not know what that will be."

Ishtar had thought he'd feel safer after the assassin was caught, and would finally be able to relax. But as he lay his head on a pillow in his father's tent that afternoon—his own tent still smelling of myrrh—sleep would not come to Ishtar for fear of all the evil people, poisonous creatures, and deadly situations that were waiting just over the next sand dune.

Rasad was right. Our God is a God of laws and rules. If those rules are broken, people are hurt. So everyone must obey all the laws all the time or face the punishment of God.

But that's impossible.

As the people of ancient times learned, no human can keep all the laws all the time. Sooner or later we mess up, and then God has to punish us.

Since we couldn't keep the laws ourselves, and because he didn't want to destroy us with his punishment, God sent his own son Jesus to take our punishment for us, just as Salamar was ready to take Ishtar's punishment at the start of their journey.

We humans used to live under law.

But now we live under grace—a kind of forgiveness we did not earn and do not deserve.

> For it is by grace you have been saved, through faith—and this not from yourselves, it is the gift of God. EPHESIANS 2:8

Thank you, Jesus!

Two Rivers

Light the first two violet candles and the pink candle.

Three mornings later, just as the sun poked up over the mountains far to their right, the caravan came to the edge of a cliff and stopped. As tired and sleepy as they were, everyone in the caravan began talking and pointing. Leaving the camel-pullers to tend the animals, they all rushed to the edge of the cliff and started shouting and singing and dancing. Ishtar pushed through the crowd to see over the edge and gasped.

Below them, stretched as far as he could see, were green fields, lush stands of palm trees, and a river as wide as the caravan was long.

Ishtar felt a hand on his shoulder and turned to see his father behind him. "We have made it across the deadlands, my son. From here on our journey will be in comfort and ease."

"No more millet?" Ishtar asked.

Salamar smiled. "No more millet. At least until the return trip," he added.

The camels were as anxious as anyone to get to the water, so Rasad decided they would take a few more hours to descend the cliffs and camp next to the river. Once there, everyone including Salamar and his brothers plunged into the cool and refreshing waters. To their left, Ishtar could see the river empty into the Akhzar Sea. To their right, he could see that the river was really *two* rivers that had joined.

"What rivers are these?" he asked his father.

Salamar looked upstream and said, "The one to the right is the Tigris. The one to the left the Euphrates. We shall have to cross them both."

Two mornings later they reached a place where Rasad said the Tigris was shallow enough to cross, but the camels all stopped and refused to step into the water. "Watch now, and learn," Kazeem said to Ishtar. The caravan was all bunched up along the shore. At the front of the line a camel-puller tugged on the first camel's reins with all his might. But the camel refused to budge.

At one point the camel-puller slipped and fell flat on his back in the mud. Everyone except the camel-puller laughed. He got up and pulled even harder. Rasad went stomping to the front of the line and yelled at the camel-puller. Ishtar couldn't hear the words, but guessed that Rasad was asking what the problem was. Finally Rasad turned to the camel and with his hands on his hips yelled two words to the beast. Immediately the camel stepped into the water and started across the river. "That is why he is *karvan-salar*," Kazeem said. "Even camels obey his commands."

Once the first animal was in, all the rest followed. "You see," Kazeem said, "just like sheep. Camels hate the water, but they hate being left behind even more."

Now between the two great rivers, the caravan headed north, enjoying the cool breezes and cool grasses of this rich land. They began traveling half at night, to follow the star, and half in the day, to see the terrain in front of them. On one of those days Ishtar saw a huge pile of rubble and some columns leaning into the sky as he practiced his horsemanship. He brought his horse next to his father's and Rasad's. "What is that?" he asked.

"The ruins of Babylon," his father said. "Once a great city."

Ishtar raised an eyebrow. "What happened?"

"We Jews were conquered by Babylon when it was ruled by Nebuchadnezzar," Rasad said. "Then you Persians, led by Cyrus, conquered Babylon. Then our Jehovah conquered your Cyrus!"

Rasad laughed and seemed quite pleased with himself as he rode away, and Ishtar was surprised to see the *karvan-salar* happy.

"Rasad is right," Salamar said. "Cyrus was moved by their God to let the Jews go home to rebuild the temple in Jerusalem."

Ishtar squinted at his father. "This is starting to sound like a history lesson."

Salamar smiled and just said, "You asked!"

"Yes, I did," Ishtar said glumly. "And I am embarrassed I did not know these things. Perhaps you should punish my teacher of history."

"You are only eleven years old," Salamar answered. "There are still one or two things you have yet to learn."

Ishtar and everyone else enjoyed this part of the trip. They bought real food from local farmers. The first time Ishtar put fresh grapes into his mouth he began to dance around and shout for the soothing taste of it. He repeated this dance threefold when he got his first taste of *khorakeh goosht*—braised meat and vegetables spiced with *zaatar*, Ishtar's favorite. Zaatar made his mouth and tongue tingle.

In only two more days they had reached the city of Seleucia. Jutting out of the ground, flanked on two sides by the Tigris River, surrounded by trees, Seleucia was even more beautiful than Amaranth, Ishtar thought. Then he caught himself and thought *almost* more beautiful. Inside the walls of the city every street and boulevard was filled with people and animals of all types, just like Amaranth. Ishtar enjoyed going from booth to booth and talking to anyone who would listen.

The people of the caravan spent a whole day in the city, eating foods from around the world such as fresh almonds and peaches, buying supplies, replacing worn out bags and blankets. Some watched entertainments like musicians from Byzantium, or a Greek play. Salamar bought new clothes for all their household, and Varta was especially happy to have a new pot.

The star did not appear the first night at Seleucia, nor the second, so the caravan was able to have a fine rest. The assassin Farad had been turned over to the local authorities. That night as they sat quietly by the fire Ishtar said, "Father, the old man, Farad, who tried to kill me. He thought he was just doing right for his family, didn't he."

Ishtar saw his father's head nodding in the firelight. "Yes, yes he did," he said. "But he went about it in the wrong way."

Several more moments passed as Ishtar thought. "Still, I hope they are not too harsh with him," he said.

On their third day in the city it began to rain, and soon everyone was huddled in their tents. Ishtar took refuge in the large tent of his father but watched the rain and lightning from the open door flaps. It was then he overheard an argument between Salamar and Rasad.

"No, no, no!" said Rasad, his face red and covered in sweat. "It is a foolish risk. We *must* travel the safe route, north through Aleppo."

"We will travel the way of the star," Salamar said forcefully, "but I am certain it will take us through Palmyra!"

Ishtar wandered over next to his father. "What are you fighting about?" he asked.

"We're not fighting," Salamar said, ignoring the breach of etiquette. "We are discussing. But this . . ." Salamar pointed at Rasad but did not finish the insult.

"What is the disagreement?" Ishtar asked.

Salamar drew a deep breath and forced himself to calm. "Rasad is insisting that we travel north, through the city of Aleppo, then west and back south along the seashore. It is a pleasant route, full of green grass and blue waters, but it will take a month longer," he finished, looking sternly at Rasad.

"Well that's ridiculous!" Ishtar said. "And what is the way *you* propose?"

"I am *insisting* that the star will take us a short way north and west, to the oasis of Palmyra, then south and west to Galilee. It is not such a pleasant route, but will cut a month off our travel."

Ishtar shrugged. "Oh," he said. "That makes sense." Then walked away.

By this time the sun had set and the rain had stopped, but clouds and lightning still filled the sky. The tent felt small and confining—which was strange since until the caravan trip he had always hated being outdoors—so Ishtar decided to go for a walk in the fresh evening air. Kazeem and Yazdan followed as he walked along the riverbank, which smelled a little like fish. As he turned away from the water Isthar looked to the sky and gasped. The clouds parted just slightly and only for a moment, but in that moment he saw the stars.

Ishtar stared for a moment, then quickly looked down to the horizon and noted the landmarks. Then he ran for his father's tent while Kazeem yelled at him to slow down. In moments he reached Salamar's side, panting.

"I saw . . . I saw the star," he said, gasping for air.

"Excellent," Salamar said. "In what direction?"

"I shall have to show you," Ishtar answered. "It is not a direction I have seen before." Ishtar dragged his father, uncles, and Rasad back to the spot by the river. He looked for his landmarks as he'd been taught, then pointed into the sky. "There," he said.

Ishtar felt his father slump slightly next to him, and heard all the others gasp. "No! It cannot be!" Rasad sputtered.

"May the gods have mercy on us," Uncle Jodhpur wheezed.

"What?" Ishtar said. "What is it?"

Salamar dropped to one knee and looked Ishtar in the eye. "Ishtar, are you *certain* you saw the star *there*? Are you *certain* it was the same star?"

"Of course," Ishtar answered as if Salamar had asked if the sun rises in the morning. "I saw the star *there* and it *was* the correct star!"

Ishtar saw a look of doubt on Rasad's face, then on the faces of his uncles. Salamar only sighed. "Then that is the direction we must go," he said. He looked at all the others. "My son is well educated, he is intelligent, and he is truthful. He is also a prince of Persia. If he says he saw the star there, then I believe him. We shall leave at once and travel through the night."

With that, all discussion was closed and the others left to start preparations. "Father, why is everyone so upset?" Isthar asked.

Salamar turned to his son. "Because the star is taking us on a very dangerous journey," he said. "The star is taking us into the wilderness of death."

God reminds us in Isaiah 55 that his way of thinking about things and doing things is not the same as ours:

> "As the heavens are higher than the earth, so are my ways higher than your ways and my thoughts than your thoughts." ISAIAH 55:9

Where we think small and limited thoughts, he thinks grand and audacious thoughts. Where we see only the immediate results of an event—as if we were seeing just the first domino in a line—he sees exactly how *every* domino will fall.

When Cyrus conquered Babylon, the Jews who lived there because they'd been captured were probably afraid of what this new king would do. But God had greater ideas. He knew where it would lead. And soon Cyrus had been so moved by God that he allowed the Jews to go home to Jerusalem and honor him.

It was like that when Jesus was born, too. Not many people really understood what was going on. They expected Jesus to act in certain ways, but God's ways were surprising.

It's like that for the caravan now, as only Ishtar knows for certain that the star is really leading them.

And it's like that for us, when the future looks scary and we don't know what's going to happen.

The point here seems clear: we need to trust God, no matter how dark the future looks, even if we don't understand.

Desert

Light the first two violet candles and the pink candle.

The whole camp mumbled and whispered, and kept glancing Ishtar's direction as they loaded the camels in the dark. The young prince couldn't make out all the words, but every so often he'd hear "We shall all be dead in three days!" or "No one has ever taken this route and lived!" and "Salamar shall kill us all, on the word of a small boy!"

The words hurt Ishtar, and he began to think maybe he hadn't seen what he thought he'd seen. Just before the caravan started out, he found his father at the front of the line. "Father, uh, I am thinking that, uh, perhaps my eyes were, uh, tricked into seeing the star. Perhaps I did not see it after all."

Salamar stared at his son for a long moment, then said, "Ishtar, I must know this for certain. Did you or did you not see the star?"

Ishtar hung his head, and that brought an instant reaction from his father. "Ishtar! Why do you hang your head in shame? Have you made the *poz dadan*? If so tell me now, so we can fix it. But," he said, softening his voice and lifting his son up to eye level, "if you truly did see the star, then I must know that as well."

Demons were fighting a war inside Ishtar's head. He *thought* he had seen the star, and was sure of it at the time, but all the voices whispering in the night, all the doubts that now crawled around inside his head . . . what if he was wrong? What if people died because he made a mistake?

Suddenly Ishtar snapped his head up and looked his father in the eye. "No!" he said loudly. "I - am - absolutely - certain."

Salamar nodded. "Very well then, it is time to go."

The two bells rang out and the caravan lumbered into motion. Ishtar waited until his own file reached him, then began walking next to Musa. There was no talking, no singing, no laughing. The entire caravan was silent except for the footsteps. Even Kazeem and Varta were especially quiet and glum.

In a few hours they reached the Euphrates River. Salamar made the dangerous decision to keep moving and cross it in the dark, so he sent the soldiers on horseback ahead to form two lines across the water, each soldier holding a torch in his hand. With Rasad in the lead to keep the camels moving, the entire caravan crossed the river between the two lines of light without incident.

On the other side of the river the camels kept moving while all the people filled every bag and pitcher they could find with water. Then they started the steep climb up to the rocky plateau.

Ishtar was riding Musa now, and looked ahead at the vast nothing in front of them. A bright moon shone above the clouds, and he could clearly see as far as the horizon a half-day's ride ahead. Other than rocks just big enough to stumble on, there was nothing. No hills, no boulders, no plants, not even many snakes or lizards. He saw only one scorpion scurry across the sand the whole first night.

The sun rose above the high clouds and Ishtar thought he was surely roasting on a spit over a fire. It was hotter here at sunrise than on the worst afternoon of the first part of the journey. Kazeem covered him in his dark blanket but it didn't help. The hot air seemed to blast up from the ground and consume him.

And the sun had only been up for five minutes.

Musa would only take five or six steps before Ishtar's mouth felt shriveled like a date, so he'd take a sip of water. Five or six steps later he'd have to take another.

"Slowly, my prince," Kazeem said. You must ration yourself against death. We will pass no water for the next five days." Ishtar watched a drop of water fall from his pouch. It evaporated to nothing before it could hit the ground.

An hour after sunrise the two bells finally rang and the caravan stopped. This time they didn't bother forming a defensive circle. "No bandit would be foolish enough to travel this desert," Kazeem said.

Varta served bits of salt with the morning millet. "Salt will make me thirsty!" Ishtar protested.

"But the heat will make you dead if you do not eat it," she answered.

Ishtar looked at Musa and wanted to give his friend some water. But Kazeem and everyone else kept warning him that the water was only for the people: the camels would have to take care of themselves.

No one had the energy to properly set up tents in the heat, so they propped them up on sticks, making just enough shade to sleep under. There being no danger from raiders, Ishtar and his guards gathered under the shade of Salamar's tent. It was good to sleep next to his father again, Ishtar thought. But there was very little sleep that day, especially when the camels began to lie down on their backs and roll in the dirt.

"They cool themselves in this way," Salamar told his son. "But it means even they are feeling the heat." There also would be no horse or sword or arrow training during this part of the trip, his father had declared.

Night finally came, but still the sky was hidden in clouds. No matter, Salamar said, they could not delay even an hour to see if the star appeared: they had to cross this desert as quickly as possible, or die. Somehow Rasad managed to keep the caravan pointed in a straight line across the nothingness.

For five days and nights it was the same: the sun baked the caravan all through the day; at night the clouds held in the heat and hid the star from view. By the third day everyone's lips and faces were dry and cracked, like the shell of a coconut. Inside Ishtar, the fear that he had been wrong grew bigger each moment.

On the fourth day the camels complained more loudly when loaded, and walked more slowly once moving. Somewhere in the middle of the night they began to moan, and soon a loud chorus of camel moans filled the desert. "They are running out of water," Ishtar's camel-puller said, and Ishtar noticed that the humps of the camels were becoming small and flabby. "One more day and they die."

Ishtar desperately wanted to give Musa a drink, but had learned by now it was important to obey his elders, who knew much more about these things than did he.

Then a *shamal* wind started to blow, hot and full of sand. It blew so hard Ishtar couldn't even hear the camels moaning. Nor could he see past Musa's head. The sand blasted his blanket, and if he didn't hold his head just right it blasted his face as well.

All through the night and into the next day Ishtar trusted that, somewhere ahead of Musa, there was a camel-puller leading the file.

On the fifth night, as the sandstorm continued, Ishtar knew he would not make it alive across this evil desert. Rumors had been passed up through the wind, rumors about a woman who went mad and tried to bake bread on a rock, but it had burned before she could eat it. Rumors about a man who had been blown off his camel and was lost forever somewhere out in the sandstorm. Rumors of camels falling down dead, and Salamar said that one might actually be true.

Just before sunrise of the fifth morning the wind finally stopped blowing, and the sand settled out of the air. And there, directly in front of them, low in the sky but shining brightly, was the star.

Ishtar had been right.

A short time later they seemed to be coming to the end of the world. The black line of the horizon drew ever closer, with nothing beyond it. Then the sky began to brighten and soon Ishtar could see it was not the edge of the world after all, it was the edge of a cliff, and beyond it a beautiful green valley.

They had made it.

As they drew close to the cliff the camels started getting restless, trying to buck off their loads. Within minutes they were all crying loudly and pulling at their ropes.

"Quickly!" the camel-pullers yelled. "Get off your animals!" Everyone including Ishtar did just that as the camel-pullers worked frantically to untie bags and bundles and saddles. As soon as they were free, the camels all ran ahead and plunged over the edge of the cliff, out of sight. Ishtar walked to the edge and looked over. There below them was a giant lake, blue and cool and clean.

Ishtar, like many others, fell to his knees and wept.

Rasad has worked a miracle, he decided. He is truly an amazing man.

It took another hour for the people to make the trek down the steep canyon path, and Ishtar wished he were safely riding Musa. But he understood that Musa had gone without water for five days in terrible heat. "You cannot stop a thirsty camel once it smells water," Kazeem had told him.

When they reached the lake everyone dove in with all their clothes on. They spent the entire day swimming, washing clothes, laughing, and feeling alive again. Throughout the day, Ishtar overheard people talking: "I guess the young prince was right," he heard, and "Ishtar knew what he was doing all along."

That afternoon the camel-pullers gathered their animals and took them back up the ridge to fetch their loads. After a day of rest, Salamar ordered the camels be properly dressed, now that they were out of the desert. Worn blankets and frayed ropes were replaced with fine Persian rugs and gold braid.

For the next two nights the star led them north, around the lake. "And what lake is this?" Ishtar asked his father as they rode, he on Musa and his father on his horse.

"It is called Galilee."

Ishtar thought a moment. "That is Greek. It means to put your trust in someone. I wonder who these Jews are going to trust."

On the second morning Ishtar was sitting by the fire, then stood and turned to see the scar-faced salt buyer he had embarrassed walking quickly toward him, sword in hand. Ishtar screamed and jumped back as Kazeem jumped forward and drew his own sword. The man stopped and looked from Ishtar to Kazeem, then down at his sword.

"Oh, sorry," he said, and dropped the sword. "I was cutting fresh palm branches and decided I could wait no longer." Ishtar was silent, unsure what the man was saying. The salt buyer cleared his throat, coughed, then finally forced himself to speak. "I came to apologize, my prince, for my behavior in Zelzele. And to thank you for forcing me to face my own sin. I . . . I have thought much about your words and my own heart since then, and decided I did not like the man I was. These last days you have proven yourself a strong and courageous young man. In the future, I will keep these lessons in my heart." The man bowed, then said, "In any case, thank you." He turned, picked up his sword, and walked away, leaving a stunned Ishtar standing by the fire.

Kazeem sheathed his sword and said, "It takes a strong man to admit his weakness."

As the caravan traveled around the lake it passed several small towns in the night, and a bigger town called Capernaum.

"Can we not stop and enjoy some good meals?" Ishtar whined to his father as the sun rose.

"Patience," Salamar kept saying. "The best is yet ahead of us. A place where they make the finest pickled fish in the world. It is for this that my mouth waters." Ishtar scrunched up his nose at the thought of pickled fish, and decided it must be something only old people liked. "Not true!" said Salamar. "It is a rare delicacy! From Taricheae they ship barrels and barrels of it to Rome, and Byzantium, and all around the world!"

"Tari-what?" Ishtar asked.

"Tari*cheae*," Salamar answered. "It is a beautiful village on the edge of the lake . . . and there it is!"

"You cannot stop a thirsty camel once it smells water," Kazeem had told Ishtar, and it's true. Camels can go for a time without water, even in the desert, but when they're desperate, nothing can stop them once they smell water.

Too often that's how we Christians are with Jesus: we wait until we're desperate before we turn to him. As long as our lives are going fine we don't mind being on our own. It isn't until something goes wrong, when life seems overwhelming and we're running on empty, that we realize we need Jesus. At that point we'll go running back to him.

And that's okay. When things go wrong our first act *should* be to call on God for help. He's always there.

But wouldn't it be better to never get to that point? Wouldn't it be better to have a healthy drink of Jesus every day, so you never get quite that desperate? Jesus thinks about you and seeks out your friendship all day every day.

Maybe that's why he called himself the "living water."

Friends

Light the first two violet candles and the pink candle.

Ishtar looked to where his father pointed from atop his horse. It just looked like another town to Ishtar, but soon they had stopped and made camp and there was, indeed, a pleasant smell of roasting fish drifting on the morning breeze.

As soon as the caravan appeared at Taricheae, townspeople came flocking out to sell their local wares. Ishtar watched as his father made several trades for various kinds of fish. He made Ishtar try each one. Some were very good, but some Ishtar thought tasted like the fur of a sweaty camel, which Ishtar was by now very familiar with.

Then Ishtar noticed a boy about his age standing on the outskirts of the camp. The boy was scanning the entire caravan, searching for something. He saw Salamar and came running up.

"Good sir! Good sir!" the boy yelled in Aramaic. "Or should I call you 'your majesty' or 'your holiness'?"

Ishtar's father smiled. "You may call me Salamar."

"Salamar, I have for you the most wonderful news!"

"Oh, and what is that?"

"Just this morning the tastiest redfish in the lake swam up to me and said he was there to give himself up for the most honorable and noble Persian man of an approaching caravan. And here you are!"

Salamar laughed a loud laugh. "And for how much did this redfish say he would sell himself before being smoked and salted?"

The boy shrugged. "Oh, only a small token of, say, five measures of fine Persian tea."

"Five measures, eh," Salamar said, stroking his beard. "And did this redfish tell you that he is really only worth *three* measures?"

Now the boy frowned and looked to the ground. "Oh no, your nobleness." Then he smiled just a little and looked up with one eye. "But he did mention that he would be willing to sacrifice his life for *four* measures, if the Persian were truly noble."

Salamar laughed again. "Then it is done!" he said, and the trade was made. "And what is your name, he who speaks to the fish?"

The boy looked up with a huge grin, as if he'd just made a new friend. "My name is Bartholomew," he said. "Bartholomew of Taricheae!"

Ishtar introduced himself and the boys became instant friends. But they had only talked a few minutes before the bell rang and the caravan started moving again—against the bitter complaints of the camels.

"Ishtar! Come now!" Kazeem called.

"Perhaps when we come back this way we can spend more time together," Ishtar said.

"It will be my great joy to show you my home, and my family," Bartholomew answered.

With that, Ishtar ran to catch up with the caravan, waving goodbye to his new friend.

It was much more pleasant walking along the green grasses of the lakeshore than the desert above. Ishtar let his mind drift back to his home in Amaranth. It seemed like a foreign place now, but he still missed it. Shouts along the caravan brought his mind back to Galilee, and he looked to where everyone was pointing.

Romans. On the top of the hill the caravan traveled the bottom of. Roman soldiers, marching north, toward Taricheae. A shudder passed through Ishtar, and he ran ahead to the front of the caravan.

"Father! You see the Romans?"

"Yes," Salamar answered. "I've been watching them for some time."

"Will they attack us?"

Salamar looked at his son and smiled. "Oh no. They may try to annoy us a bit since we're in their territory, but they know better than to cause any real trouble."

Every Persian child knew the stories of how the great Roman senator Cassius had dared to attack Persia fifty years before, and had been soundly beaten. A few years later Mark Antony had tried it again and also suffered a humiliating defeat. Since then, the Romans and Persians had enjoyed a shaky peace, but not without some occasional harassment on both sides. Ishtar returned to Musa and looked behind them as he climbed on the camel's back. In the distance he saw a tall plume of smoke rising, and he wondered what was on fire.

The caravan was still plodding ahead a few hours later as the sun set. Salamar looked for the star but couldn't see it. Nor could his brothers. Nor could Ishtar. Salamar sighed.

"Then we camp here tonight, and wait for it to join us again."

"Here," it turned out, was just outside the city of Tiberius, still on the edge of the lake. The following day, nearly everyone on the caravan enjoyed shopping there, but Salamar returned early, deep in thought.

"What is it, Father?" Ishtar asked.

"I heard news in the city. The Romans began a series of raids yesterday, from Jerusalem all the way north to Aleppo." He turned and looked at his son. "They even destroyed many caravans along the trade routes, and took their goods as 'taxes.' And they took many people as slaves."

Rasad was nearby, tending to a camel's hoof. "I would spit in the face of a Roman before I let him take me!"

"And then you would be dead," Salamar said as a matter of fact.

"Just wait until the Messiah comes!" Rasad answered.

"Messiah?" Ishtar asked. "Some men we ate with talked about that. What is *messiah*?"

"He will be our deliverer," Rasad said. "One day our Messiah shall come and destroy these Romans, and all other enemies of Israel!"

Rasad seemed to be getting very upset and Ishtar turned back to his father.

"Did the Romans get any of our friends from the caravans we passed?" Ishtar asked.

Salamar shook his head. "I do not know. But what I *do* know is this: if we had followed Rasad's plan of traveling north, or even my plan to go through Palmyra, the Romans would have surely stopped us and would not have hesitated to steal our cargo. By following you and the star," he said as he turned and looked at Ishtar, "we were saved."

For five more days they camped at Tiberius. On the second day it was decided that Rasad had fulfilled his duties, and Ishtar accompanied his father to where the man was packing his camels.

"Are you anxious to get home, Rasad?" Salamar asked.

"Indeed. I should have a brand new grandchild waiting for me, and six others I cannot wait to hug!"

Ishtar was surprised. "You have grandchildren?"

"Two boys and four girls," Rasad answered with a huge grin, "plus an unknown! It is the joy of my life to spoil them thoroughly."

Ishtar was stunned. Just two days before, this same man had looked like he was ready to go to war with Rome. Ishtar shook his head slowly. "I have learned much from you on this journey, Rasad. And I continue to learn even now."

Rasad put his hand on the boy's shoulder. "We have learned from each other, young prince," he said quietly.

On the fifth day the star appeared again and led them south, along the Jordan River, toward the Sea of Death. Three days after that they reached a city named Jericho. Like most of the other places they passed, Ishtar didn't think this was much of a city, compared to his home of Amaranth, but its hills were covered in cool grasses and the city itself was full of tall palm trees.

Once again the star left the caravan, though Salamar sent Ishtar out every night to look for it. Ishtar was happy for the days of rest and recovery, and for the new clothes and better foods these days brought. He still had to take his riding and fighting lessons in the mornings, but the afternoons were free for talking with others in the city, exploring the shops and shores of Jericho, and flying his kite up on the hillside.

On one particularly fine day, full of blue skies and a stiff breeze, Ishtar was flying his kite when he heard his father calling. He handed the string to Kazeem, who acted as if the boy had handed him a rat instead. Then Ishtar ran to his father's tent where Salamar sat outside with a strange looking man and a boy.

"Yes, Father," he said.

Salamar introduced the boy. "This is Jotham of Jericho. He is our guest. Treat him as such."

That was all the instruction Ishtar needed. He bowed deeply to Jotham and said, "May the sheep on a thousand hilltops grace your father's flock, and may you find peace and joy among the tents of my father."

Jotham returned the bow, and then Ishtar introduced himself. "I am Ishtar of Persia. It will be my honor to be your host on this most glorious day!"

With the formalities of protocol taken care of, the two boys ran off among the tents and camels, Ishtar leading the way. Even though they were in Jotham's own land, and even near the town of his birth, Ishtar knew it was his duty to act as host as long as they were in the camp of his father.

As they passed Kazeem, Ishtar introduced him. "Jotham, this is my body . . . my friend, Kazeem."

"It is my honor to meet you," Jotham said, then threw his head back and stared up into the sky. "What *is* that thing?" he asked, pointing to the cloth that flew.

Ishtar looked up. "It is a kite," he said plainly. "It flies on the breath of the god of wind."

Ishtar then gave Jotham a tour of the camp, though it seemed Jotham was more interested in the kite overhead.

"This is my uncle Jodhpur's tent," Ishtar said, and Jotham gaped at the fine stitchery and colorful designs. "He comes from the house of Rajasthan." Ishtar knew this would impress the other boy. After all, who didn't know the daring stories of the house of Rajasthan?

They passed the smaller tents surrounding the large one of Ishtar's uncle, each of which was home to three or four women. "Those are my uncle's favorite wives," he said. "He left the rest at home. My own father is very protective of them, and calls them his daughters."

"Where *is* home?" Jotham asked.

"We come from Amaranth. And you are from Jericho, correct?"

"Well, yes, that is where I was born. But my family are shepherds, and we live wherever the grazing is best or there is a market for our sheep and wool."

"Where is your family now?" Ishtar asked as they reached his tent and sat in the shade.

And so Jotham told him a story. He told how he found his father's camp deserted, and about finding his own grave. He told how he had been picked up by another family of shepherds, about how the evil Decha of Megiddo had kidnapped him and tried to sell Jotham into slavery, and about his new friend Nathan—the strange looking man—who dressed as a fool and rescued him in En Gedi. He told of fleeing to Qumran, and about a man named Silas being killed, right here in Jericho. Then he talked about a priest named Zechariah and his wife, Elizabeth, and how he, Jotham of Jericho, was going to be the cousin of a baby named Jesus. He finished his story with a tale of a second rescue by Nathan, and how a man named Caleb had killed most of Decha's men in a fierce battle.

When Jotham finished telling his story, Ishtar sat cross-legged with his head bowed. After several seconds Jotham said, "Ishtar, what is wrong?"

Ishtar spoke slowly, without raising his head. "I hang my head in shame for you, Jotham of Jericho."

Ishtar had been right!

Though everyone in the caravan thought he was crazy, and even his father was uneasy about it, it turned out that Ishtar was the only one who knew what direction the caravan should travel. But he was so scared of what everyone else would think that he almost didn't follow what he knew to be true.

We are so much like that! Many times we know the *right* thing to do, or say, or not do, but we're so afraid of what our "friends" will think of us that we ignore that knowledge.

> Every prudent man acts out of knowledge, but a fool exposes his folly.
>
> PROVERBS 13:16

Jesus' words and actions in the Gospels, and his very real presence in our lives, is the "star" we follow. We must follow that star even if others make fun of us, or the consequences could be disastrous.

Jotham's Journey

Light the first two violet candles and the pink candle.

Jotham appeared shocked. "Wh-why?" he asked. "Because many men were killed on my account?"

Ishtar sucked in his breath, then slowly shook his head. "No," he said. "I am embarrassed for you because you have to make up stories to impress me. In my land that is called the *poz dadan*, the building of a false image."

"Ishtar," Jotham said through his teeth, his anger evident, "everything I have told you is the truth!"

Ishtar just shook his head slowly again, and avoided looking at Jotham.

Finally Jotham pulled Ishtar to his feet and said, "Follow me!"

Nathan and Salamar were sitting around a fire drinking tea as Jotham and Ishtar approached. Salamar was just saying, "No matter what, we will need to stop in Jerusalem to pay respects to your elders. And I have sent men ahead to inquire about the new king." Then he saw Ishtar and frowned. "Ishtar! Why do you hang your head in shame?"

Ishtar fidgeted, not wanting to tell on his friend. "Ishtar! Answer!" his father commanded.

Slowly, painfully, Ishtar said, "My friend Jotham has made the *poz dadan*."

Ishtar's father looked from Jotham to Nathan and back. Then to his son said, "What did he tell you?"

Ishtar gave a brief summary, now trying to make it sound less preposterous, in order to keep Jotham's punishment to a minimum. When he finished, Nathan began laughing, and laughed so hard he fell on his side and knocked over the pitcher of tea. "Ishtar," he said, wiping his eyes, "everything Jotham told you is absolutely true!"

Ishtar's eyes grew as wide as grapefruit. "But this cannot be . . ." he said, slumping to the ground. "My friend Jotham is no older than myself . . . to have such adventures!" Ishtar looked at Jotham like he was a holy man, but now it was Jotham who hung his head.

"It is true," he said, "that much has happened to me in the last days. But all of this happened, Ishtar, because I did a bad thing. Nathan's friend Silas lives no more because of my disobedience."

It was quiet for a moment, then Salamar said, "It is a wise man who recognizes the fruits of his errors. It is a *compassionate* man who regrets that fruit. You are truly becoming a man, Jotham of Jericho."

Jotham smiled his thanks to Salamar, then Nathan said, "Jotham, my friend Salamar and his caravan are headed west, toward Jerusalem. He has agreed to take you as far as his course allows." Ishtar looked at his father for confirmation. When his father nodded, Ishtar grinned a wide grin. He not only had a new friend, but that friend would be traveling with them. Now nothing could possibly spoil this glorious journey!

That night a huge banquet was held in Nathan's honor. He and Salamar told many boring stories about their youth. "In celebration of old warriors reunited," Salamar had told the assembly at the beginning of the meal. "And to thank the gods that my friend is safe and well."

"There *is* only one God, you know," Ishtar heard Nathan say, a mischievous grin on his lips. Salamar had laughed and said, "So there is for you, my brother. And perhaps, so shall there one day be for me." Ishtar could see that it was an old game the two played, but of course it was ridiculous that his father would ever think there to be only one god. Salamar presented Nathan with the gift of the scroll, and Nathan was most pleased. His uncle's wives even performed a dance for entertainment.

Late in the evening Kazeem led Ishtar and Jotham back to Ishtar's tent for bed. "I believe I will like having you travel with us," Ishtar said as they lay watching the stars.

"I believe I will, too," Jotham said. A moment later he asked, "Why are you in Palestine? Where are you going?"

"We follow the stars," Ishtar said. "My father and uncles are the Royal Astronomers for His Majesty Sheik Konarak of Amaranth."

Jotham stared at Ishtar in astonishment. "Your father and uncles are *royalty?!*"

Ishtar laughed. "No, not royalty, but high government officials." Then he added, "Well, in our country I guess it's the same thing."

Jotham thought for a moment. "Then you are royalty, too!"

Ishtar didn't want to answer, but knew it would be impolite not to. "I . . . I am . . . sort of a . . . prince?" He said it as if apologizing for some misdeed.

"A *prince!*" Jotham shouted. He thought for several moments then said, "This afternoon, when you introduced Kazeem. You started to say he's your bodyguard, didn't you?"

Ishtar nodded slightly. He had never in his eleven years realized what a privileged life he led until he began meeting people who were not so fortunate.

"Why are you here?" Jotham asked.

Ishtar told Jotham the story of finding the star, and bringing a message and gifts from the sheik.

Jotham scrunched up his face. "A message for *whom*?" he asked.

"Why, for your new king, of course," Ishtar answered.

"*What* new king?"

Ishtar raised up on one arm and stared at his friend. "The new king that is soon to be born to your people! Surely you know of this great thing."

Jotham shook his head slowly, looking lost. "I . . . I don't know . . ." he stammered. Then his eyes grew wide and he shouted, "The Messiah!"

"Messiah?" Ishtar said.

"Yes, the Messiah I told you about. The one whose cousin I will be!"

"It is as if the gods wanted us to meet!" Ishtar said.

"Maybe *he* did," Jotham answered. "But I still do not understand why you are here."

"We bring greetings and gifts to your new king. Gold, frankincense, and myrrh."

As soon as he said it, Ishtar realized he shouldn't have, but Jotham just shrugged.

"Why *those* gifts?"

"Gold because he is a king. Frankincense because it is the finest and most expensive fragrance of our country. And myrrh because it has many uses, and is also an expensive product of our country."

After that the two talked excitedly through the night.

Early the next morning, before the sun was even up, Kazeem woke the two boys. "We are leaving," he said. "We must find new pasture." The boys both knew it was impolite for a large caravan to stay too long outside a town and use up all the feed. They barely had time to get dressed and devour some meat and cheese before all the tents were down and packed onto camels.

Jotham gave Nathan a long hug goodbye while Ishtar pretended to be checking Musa's straps.

"Jehovah willing, we shall see each other again soon," Nathan said. Then he turned to Ishtar and added, "Perhaps I shall have a chance to get to know you better someday."

"It would be a blessing on my house," Ishtar replied, even though he didn't have a house of his own yet.

Just as the sun rose behind them, casting long shadows off their feet, the caravan molded itself smoothly into a single line headed away from Jericho, and into the hills of Judea, where Salamar knew of a meadow where they could wait for the star.

As the two boys walked beside Musa, Jotham looked at all the women in the caravan and said, "Ishtar, is your mother among the wives of your father?"

Ishtar felt his throat tighten. "My mother is not among the living," he said. "She died when I was born. She was my father's first wife, and he has never taken another."

Jotham seemed to want to know more, but didn't ask, and Ishtar was glad of it.

All day the caravan trudged up the steep path into the hills and Ishtar was deep in thought most of the way. They ate their lunch as they walked, and Ishtar explained to Jotham how you never, ever stop a caravan unless you're ready to water the camels.

Finally they reached a cool meadow with a small stream. The sun was just beginning to set and the tents were quickly raised. Ishtar was grateful when they could finally sit by a fire and eat some dinner. Salamar and his brothers didn't eat, but instead stood around with their instruments looking into the sky.

Ishtar fell into deep thought again as he stared into the fire. He didn't even notice that Jotham had wandered off until Salamar came and sat to eat his dinner in the place where Jotham had been. He looked about and saw Jotham a short distance from the camp, sitting at the base of a lone olive tree and staring into the sky.

"You are quiet this evening, my son. Is there trouble in your heart?"

Ishtar hesitated, then said, "In my heart, and in my head."

"Tell me of this trouble."

Ishtar squirmed, then said, "Father, what happened when I was born?"

Salamar stopped with his food halfway to his mouth. He put it back down and spent several moments wiping his hands on a cloth.

"It is a very difficult thing for me to speak of." After several more moments he added, "But you have a right to know. When you were born there was a problem and you could not come out of your mother in the normal way. The physician tried to save both you and your mother, but alas, your mother was injured too badly. But it was not your fault."

Ishtar thought about this for a long moment then asked, "And what of Kazeem? Why has he been my bodyguard from that day?"

Salamar looked to where Kazeem stood guard and nodded to him. "The time has come," he said. Kazeem sat next to Ishtar and took a deep breath. "You mother, father, and I were all close friends," he said. "When the physician said there was a problem, your mother told him to save you no matter what. She knew your father would have many other responsibilities, so she looked to me and made me promise that I would keep you safe until you were a man."

Ishtar thought about that a long time, then said, "So you are not a slave, nor even a servant. You . . . you are truly a friend to my father, and to me."

Kazeem looked at Salamar for permission, then back to Ishtar. "Yes, that is the truth," he said.

Ishtar stared back into the fire and pondered these things in his heart.

Salamar finished his meal quietly, then stood with a sigh, and walked away. From a distance Ishtar heard his father say something about a boy sitting alone, but he was thinking so hard about his mother, father, and Kazeem that he ignored it. He was just forming some questions when he heard his father shouting. Ishtar looked up and saw that the entire caravan was scrambling to take down the tents and load the camels. "We leave at once!" he heard echoed around the camp. Ishtar set his questions aside and began to help, as he knew his father would want. He had for the moment forgotten all about Jotham until his new friend came running up, crying.

"Jotham! What is it? What's happening?" Ishtar yelled over the excitement in the camp.

"I do not know!" Jotham said. "All I did was look at a star and everyone got upset!"

Ishtar nodded knowingly, patted his friend on the shoulder, and said, "You get a lot of that around here."

If we still lived in the garden of Eden, everything would be perfect. There would be no pain, no hunger, no death, no hurt.

But God had to banish Adam and Eve from the garden as a consequence of their self-centeredness, and things have never been perfect since then.

So we live in a world where there's pain, and hunger, and death, and hurt. It helps us bear all that when we at least have someone who comforts us, and provides for us, and kisses our wounds.

Ishtar is sad that he has no mother, and nothing can ever make that pain go away entirely. But besides his father, Ishtar's mother also left Kazeem to watch over and care for him in every way. She left him to be a bodyguard and a friend to Ishtar.

That's exactly what God did for us when he sent Jesus to be our closest friend, and then the Holy Spirit to guard us.

> Praise be to the God and Father of our Lord Jesus Christ, the Father of compassion and the God of all comfort . . . 2 CORINTHIANS 1:3

Decha of Megiddo

Light the first two violet candles and the pink candle.

Ishtar sat on his golden throne, his loyal and loving subjects shouting his . . . He jerked awake. "What's going on here!" he shouted. It took a few moments before he realized he was riding atop Musa, and sat behind Jotham.

"Good morning, friend," Jotham said. "It is daylight and we still travel toward Jerusalem. Your servant Kazeem lifted us up here in the night."

"He is not a servant," Ishtar said, then looked upward. "The star is gone. I will speak with my father." He slid down off the camel and ran forward along the caravan, which swayed slowly back and forth in the sun. He spoke with his father, then returned to Jotham.

"My father said we followed the star all night," Ishtar reported as he walked alongside Musa. "They set their sights on it and follow its course still."

The caravan continued on for a time and then stopped at a narrow plateau between the rocky hills. Only a few tents for the women were put up. All the men lay down to sleep out in the open. Jotham and Ishtar weren't tired, though, since they'd slept on the camel all night, so they set about exploring the desert hills. It was Kazeem's turn to sleep, so Yazdan followed them.

The boys found plenty to do. They chased scorpions and snakes—except for the ones they knew to be dangerous—and tried to catch the few small animals that they saw. But then, just before noon, they saw a rare sight. A silver fox was prowling around the bushes, stalking a hare a few feet away. Carefully, Jotham and Ishtar worked their way through the brush, trying to sneak up on the fox. They didn't get closer than twenty feet before it heard them and took off running.

The two boys went after the fox, leaping over scrub brush and rocks, laughing all the way. They scrambled up some boulders taller than a camel. Ishtar glanced around and realized he'd lost Yazdan in the maze. But then he spied the fox, sitting at the top of the hill and, as if on cue, both boys leaped at it, missing it by inches. Ishtar started to follow it down the other side when Jotham suddenly screamed and grabbed him by the collar.

"Decha!" Jotham screamed. Ishtar screamed too, though he wasn't really sure why. Then he looked where his friend was pointing. There, sitting on a rock by a fire eating his breakfast, was a man who looked like all the nightmares that had ever terrified Ishtar's brain.

Farther down the hill Ishtar saw two men jump up from where they'd been sleeping.

"Run!" Jotham yelled, and the two boys took off back down the hill toward the caravan. Their feet pounded the ground, sometimes slipping on loose rocks. Jotham was in the lead and looked back behind them. "They're catching up!" he yelled, and Ishtar ran faster. They came around a hill and just as he ran between two clumps of brush Ishtar hollered as the ground disappeared beneath his feet. He fell into a dark hole and landed with a thud that hurt his ankle. He looked up and saw that the hole was just big enough for him to fall through. When he stood, it was short enough that his head could stick up through it, which he did.

"Yech!" he exclaimed.

Jotham looked back where they had come from, then jumped on top of Ishtar's shoulders, driving him back into the hole. The two boys slammed into the floor of a cave. Ishtar's ankle twisted again and he started to protest but Jotham quickly clamped his hand over his friend's face. Both boys listened as a man's running feet passed the cave and kept going. After a few moments, Jotham let go of Ishtar.

"Ow!" Ishtar yelled. "That hurt!"

"Trust me," Jotham said, panting, "it would hurt a great deal more if Decha were to catch us."

Jotham thought for a moment, then tore a piece off his tunic and wrapped it around a stick. With a piece of metal and a stone, he lit the cloth on fire, which seemed like magic to Ishtar.

"What are you doing?" Ishtar asked.

"We're going to follow this tunnel," Jotham said, not realizing that wasn't the question Ishtar was asking.

"We're *what*?"

"We cannot go back outside," Jotham continued. "Decha and his men have probably already figured out we did not make it back to the caravan and are hiding somewhere. They will be searching the area above us."

Ishtar looked at the rock ceiling over their heads and shuddered. "Then let us move quickly," he said. "Which direction shall we go?"

Jotham looked back and forth, then turned to his left. "This way," he said. "And do not look directly at the torch or you will not be able to see in the dark."

"I cannot see in the dark in any event," Ishtar answered.

"When looking in the dark, do not look where you want to look. Look just to the side of the thing and you will see it. It is how Jehovah made our eyes to work."

Ishtar didn't comment about Jehovah, but discovered he really could see in the dark by looking to the side of the thing he wanted to see.

Slowly they climbed along the jagged edges of the tunnel with Jotham in the lead. Ishtar was terrified—never in his life had he been more than a few paces away from Kazeem. But he followed his new friend, favoring his hurt ankle. All of a sudden the floor of the tunnel leveled out and sloped downhill.

The boys edged their way forward, and Ishtar's heart pounded in his chest, thinking that maybe this wasn't such a good idea. He was just about to say they should turn back when a man's voice came haunting them through the cave.

"Little one," came the faint but evil voice. Ishtar wondered for a moment who he was talking to. "Little one! Come back to me! I am going to kill you, little one! You may run, but I am going to catch you and kill you!"

"It's Decha," Jotham whispered, close to Ishtar's ear. Ishtar stared at Jotham in the firelight and wondered what he could have done to make the thief so mad.

"Friend of the little one," came the voice again. "Listen to me! I will not harm you! Bring your friend to me and I shall spare your life!"

Jotham's eyes grew wide and he looked at Ishtar. *I would never do such a thing!* Ishtar thought. He shook his head at Jotham, who smiled back, then they ran on, Ishtar on Jotham's heels, his ankle suddenly feeling much better. They passed through an archway cut into the rock and Ishtar saw it was covered with writings in several languages but he only had time to read the word "death" in Greek. A moment later they skidded to a stop.

"It is death!" Ishtar cried.

"Run!" Jotham shouted.

But both boys just stood there, heaving great, terrified breaths, transfixed by what they saw.

"We must leave this place," Ishtar cried. But neither of them could move. They inched their way forward. Cut into the walls of the cave in front of them, as far as the boys could see, were small alcoves. And in each alcove was a dead body wrapped in a cloth.

"Who would do such a terrible thing?" Ishtar asked, his nose scrunched in disgust.

"*What* terrible thing." Jotham panted, his own face twisted in horror at the sight.

"To put dead bodies in a cave with no sarcophagus?"

"What's a sacrifagust?"

"Sarcophagus," Ishtar corrected. "The burial box of the dead."

"I've never seen anyone buried in a box before. My people just wrap dead ones in burial cloths, and cover them with spices."

Ishtar thought this was pretty crude and very cruel, but didn't say anything more. The boys realized that Decha could reach them at any moment, and started up the tunnel again. After a few minutes, the evil voice returned, a little louder this time.

"Little one, look!" it said. "It is the bodies of your ancestors! What a good place for you to die!" Then there came a screeching, evil laugh and Ishtar ran just a little faster.

Jotham and Ishtar ran for what seemed like hours. They were almost as afraid of the dead bodies as they were of the evil voice that slithered through the dark every few minutes. Finally the tunnel ended in a huge room filled with more carvings. Jotham's torch was getting short now, and he tore another length from his tunic.

The room reminded Ishtar of the throne room back at the palace. All around its walls were cut tall archways that led to other tunnels. The archways were decorated with carved images of ancient ancestors. One was of a man walking between two walls of water. Another showed a man being spit out by a great fish.

Then, in the dimming light, they came across a flat, white stone with writing on it, and Ishtar gasped. Jotham looked at him in amazement. "You can *read* this?"

"Yes," Ishtar said, barely able to whisper. "It says, 'We wait in peace, for this is the place where the Messiah shall come to earth!'"

At that moment the voice of the devil cut through the dark. "I am here, little one," Decha hissed like a snake.

Jotham screamed and spun around in terror. In the orange light of the torch Ishtar saw Decha's face only inches away from his friend.

"Yes, I am here," Decha hissed again. "And now you are finally mine!"

Decha grabbed the front of Jotham's tunic, but Jotham plunged his torch square into the ugly man's face. Decha screamed and let go, holding his face in his hands.

"Run!" Jotham commanded Ishtar, and the two boys took off down one of the side tunnels. Behind them they could hear Decha cursing and yelling more threats.

Ishtar was running so fast it reminded him of the camels when they smelled water. The torch was getting low again and barely lit the path ahead. A moment later the tunnel turned but the boys didn't and they crashed headfirst into a skeleton hanging in an alcove. They both fell to the ground, the bones of some long-dead merchant or priest crashing down around them like a cage.

Ishtar screamed and began thrashing about like a fish out of water. Jotham just stood to his feet and threw aside the bones. "That's *it!*" he yelled. "I can't take this anymore!"

With that, he picked up the torch and started back up the tunnel, toward Decha.

"Where are you going?" Ishtar cried in panic.

"I'm going to kill Decha!"

"You're *what*?" Ishtar yelled.

And as Jotham and the light moved away into the darkness, Ishtar had to make a decision.

Despite his best intentions, Ishtar once again finds himself lost and separated from his bodyguard.

Despite our best intentions, we all sometimes make mistakes, or do things we know we shouldn't, which separates us from the One who helps and protects us.

All it takes to find him again is to realize we were wrong, ask his forgiveness, and cry for help.

> The LORD is near to all who call on him, to all who call on him in truth.
>
> PSALM 145:18

Courage

Light the first two violet candles and the pink candle.

Jotham stopped and turned back toward his friend. "I'm going to kill Decha," he repeated. "I'm sick and tired of running away!" Then he picked up a bone from the skeleton and threw it as hard as he could up the tunnel as he yelled, "I'm not scared of jackals anymore!" Then he headed back up toward Decha.

Ishtar shivered in fear. He was all alone, sitting in the bones of the dead, with his friend and the light moving away, and now Jotham had said something about there being jackals. He felt his insides shaking in panic. Then remembered all the dangerous situations he had lived through on the caravan trip. How he had faced death so many times and survived. "I will not be afraid!" he whispered. Then he pushed the bones aside, stood, and marched off to catch up with Jotham.

He found him a short ways up the tunnel.

Standing outside the light of the torch, Ishtar saw that Decha had captured Jotham and held him in an arm lock. "Who do you think you are to resist me so?" Decha hissed. Ishtar looked around frantically for a weapon of some sort. "Am I not the great Decha of Megiddo?" Ishtar spotted the bone Jotham had thrown and dove for it. "Am I not five times your size? Am I not the most—" And with that, Ishtar smacked Decha on the back of the head using one of his sword-fighting moves. The thief slumped to the floor. When he turned, Jotham's face looked a bit shocked.

"Well, I could not let him hurt my best of all friends!" Ishtar exclaimed. Jotham grinned, but then his face returned to fear. Coming up the tunnel behind Ishtar were two torches, carried by Decha's two henchmen.

"Come, we must find a way out of this place," Jotham said. He picked up the torch, then the two boys headed up the tunnel once more. They ran as fast as they could with only the dim torchlight, not wanting to smash into another wall. After a few moments they heard Decha roar in anger, and they knew they had only a few minutes before the demons would catch up to them.

That's when they heard the voices.

Faintly at first, then louder. In the dark it sounded like wind echoing off the walls. But after listening very closely, Ishtar eventually decided it was the voices of men!

"Ishtar! Listen!" Jotham commanded.

"I *have* been listening," he exclaimed. "Let us go at once!"

The boys turned down another tunnel toward the voices. They turned another corner and gasped. There was light ahead! They continued on and with each step the light got brighter. Then they rounded one last bend and saw a beautiful sight: an opening in the end of the tunnel, with two men silhouetted against the blue sky outside. The men had their backs to the boys, and were just getting ready to roll a large stone across the entrance to the cave.

"Stop!" Jotham shouted, "Wait!"

The two men jumped three feet into the air and screamed the scream of men frightened to death. They turned and ran away from the tunnel, dropping instantly out of sight down a slope. Jotham and Ishtar didn't care about the men, they just wanted out. Running at full speed they headed for the opening to the cave. But just before they got there, a huge man stepped squarely into the center of the opening and blocked their way.

Now it was the boys who screamed the scream of frightened men. They dug their heels in and a shower of dirt flew ahead of them as they slid to a stop. "Who is there!" the voice demanded, low and loud.

"It is Jotham of Jericho, and his friend Ishtar!"

"Are you of the living or of the dead?" the voice asked.

"We are of the living," Jotham answered, "though not for long if you do not allow your servants to leave this awful place!"

"Come then," the voice answered, "or be locked in with the dead!"

Jotham and Ishtar wasted no time scrambling through the opening and out into the fresh air and bright sunshine. Then they turned and began pushing on the stone and yelling at the man. "Hurry, help us!" they yelled. "A devil follows us!"

With the man's help, the two boys rolled the stone across the opening to the cave. At the last second Decha's hand shot through the opening and grabbed the stone, trying to push it back. The weight of the stone and the strength of the man were too much, and Decha screamed from inside the tunnel as the stone rolled closed, smashing his hand.

Jotham and Ishtar turned and leaned back against the stone, their eyes closed, panting like thirsty dogs. After a few moments Ishtar opened his eyes and what he saw shocked him. Because there, on the other side of the valley, sitting atop a hill like the crown on the head of Sheik Konarak, sat a city more beautiful than Amaranth.

"Jerusalem!" Jotham gasped.

An hour later Ishtar felt like he was home. He and Jotham were sitting at the center of a rich house, at the edge of a pool, their feet dangling in the water, eating coconuts and dates.

"And what is it you wait for, Simeon?" Jotham asked, slurping some coconut juice. Simeon was much older than the boys had first thought upon seeing his silhouette, and much nicer too. He had just been explaining to them how he helped bury the bodies of the dead saints while he waited.

"I wait," he said, "for the coming of the Messiah."

Once they had convinced Simeon that they were not ghosts, Jotham and Ishtar had quickly explained to him how they had come to be lost in the tunnels. With eyes so kind they reminded Ishtar of his father, Simeon had given them some water, then led them here to his own villa where he ordered them fed. He also sent a rider with a message for Ishtar's father.

"But what do you *mean* that you wait?" Jotham asked again.

Simeon told a long story about the voice of a god telling him he wouldn't die until the 'day of Israel's consolation.'" Ishtar thought the man must be mad—only in stories do gods talk to people. Then Jotham asked, "Does that mean the coming of the Messiah?"

Simeon nodded. "Yes, it does."

Jotham pulled his feet up out of the water and walked over to stand next to the man. "Simeon," he said softly, "I think perhaps I should tell you a secret."

It took several minutes for Jotham to tell his story, and Simeon seemed excited, but Ishtar still didn't understand. "What are you talking about?" he asked.

Jotham turned to his friend. "We're talking about my cousin, Jesus. He's the Messiah!"

"Which means what?" Ishtar asked.

"It means," Simeon stepped in, "that Jotham's cousin is not just a king, but God himself. It means he's coming to save the world."

Ishtar laughed. "That's ridiculous!" he said. When the other two didn't even smile, Ishtar stopped laughing and said, "Well, a man can't be a god and, even if he could, no one god is powerful enough to save the whole *world!* And save them from what?"

Ishtar still dangled his feet in the water, so Simeon pulled his tunic up over his knees and sat down next to him. "As this water washes my feet," Simeon said, "so shall the Messiah wash us all of our sins." And then he told Ishtar the most incredible stories the young prince had ever heard. Stories of Noah, Abraham, Moses, and David.

God had promised that Simeon would not die until he had seen the Messiah:

> Now there was a man in Jerusalem called Simeon, who was righteous and devout. He was waiting for the consolation of Israel, and the Holy Spirit was upon him. It had been revealed to him by the Holy Spirit that he would not die before he had seen the Lord's Christ. Luke 2:25–26

And so Simeon waited—maybe for many years—until Jesus was born and that promise could be fulfilled.

I wonder how *we'd* react if God told us there was a miracle coming, and promised us a chance to watch it happen?

Oh, wait a minute. He did.

God promised us that we can see the miracle of Jesus, and have him in our lives as savior and friend, at any moment we choose. He promised that when we call on the name of Jesus, he will be there.

Simeon waited for years to see the promise fulfilled. We don't have to wait at all.

Tabitha's Travels

Light the first two violet candles and the pink candle.

My friend," the man in the dirty tunic said, "can I interest you in a bit of baklava?" Jotham looked at Ishtar, who then looked at the pastry the man held out. Ishtar gave a slight shake of the head and Jotham said, "No, thank you." They pushed on through the crowd, trying to look into every crack and alley for a sign of Jotham's father.

"You are missing a rare delicacy!" the man in the dirty tunic yelled after them. The two boys ignored him, knowing the unwritten rules of haggling did not require them to respond.

Jerusalem didn't seem so beautiful now that Ishtar was in it. The air was foul with the stench of manure and sweat, and red-faced men pulled camels and goats and donkeys through the narrow, winding streets. There were shops everywhere, and you could buy anything, but it wasn't the wide boulevards and organized markets of Amaranth.

Ishtar kept looking around nervously. Never in his life had he been away from Kazeem or some other bodyguard for more than a few minutes, yet here he was alone in a big city. He kept telling himself that no one knew who he was, and he was dressed in an ordinary tunic. But still . . .

"What is *baklava*?" Jotham asked.

"It is a sweet and flaky pastry that is full of honey and nuts. It is the best of my people."

"So why didn't we get some?"

"Because that which the man offered was camel dung compared to *real* baklava. Besides," he said as he continued to watch faces go by, "we have no money."

They continued searching. Ishtar could only guess at what Jotham's family looked like, of course. But two sets of eyes are better than one.

"Is that him?" Ishtar asked, pointing to a middle-aged man with a beard. Jotham looked, then sighed as he said, "No. But it is a very close likeness."

Simeon was searching another part of the city. With only a description of Jotham's family it would be difficult, but Jotham had said that if his family was to be found, Simeon could find them.

The two boys had enjoyed their time with Simeon. They had talked late into the night about the Messiah. Simeon kept saying, "You are *sure* that Ishtar's father follows a rising star?" Then a few moments later he'd say, "Are you *sure* that Nathan said the time is close?" Jotham and Ishtar would nod their heads rapidly each time and say, "Yes, yes, most assuredly!"

"Ishtar look!"

Ishtar raised his head to look where Jotham was pointing. Over the top of the city wall they could see a huge caravan descending from the wilderness of Judea to the Kidron Valley. "It is my father," Ishtar yelled. Together the boys ran out the Lion's Gate in the city wall and met up with the caravan just as it reached the bottom of the valley.

"Father!" Ishtar cried when he saw him. The two hugged for a long time, then Ishtar hugged Kazeem and Varta and anyone else that would let him. He had much explaining and apologizing to do.

"It was as if you were born again," Salamar said, "when the servant of Simeon rode to our camp and told me you were alive!" He told how the entire caravan—even the women—had spent the day searching every rock and bush in the desert, and how he had sent for Nathan to help.

Salamar took Ishtar by the shoulders and stood him up straight, staring at him in the eye. "What's wrong, Father?" Ishtar asked.

"Kazeem may call me mad," Salamar said, "but I'd swear by the gods that you've grown half a cubit since we left home!"

"It is true," Varta said. "I've had to lengthen his trousers twice on this journey."

Just then Simeon walked up and Jotham introduced him. "I am in your debt," Salamar told him, "for caring for my son. May your God favor you richly for your kindness."

Simeon reported finding no trace of Jotham's family, then Salamar said, "Jotham, you are welcome to stay with our caravan if you would like. We will camp here tonight. Your King Herod heard my men were asking questions and sent word demanding we go and speak with him."

Jotham asked if Ishtar could help him search the city some more. "No, that will not be possible," Salamar said. "His place is at my side as I visit your king."

After Jotham had left to continue his search, Salamar hugged Ishtar again. "You scared me, my son. You must never run off and leave your bodyguards like that again."

"Yes father. I mean, no father. It just kind of . . . happened."

"Such things happen with boys. But you have greater responsibility than most. And the most important of your responsibilities is to stay alive." Salamar said this with a smile to show he wasn't angry. "Now, we must dress to visit Herod. You'll find new clothes waiting in your tent."

Some time later, after Ishtar had washed and changed into his new trousers and tunic—green and black with gold braid—he headed back to his father's tent. Salamar, Jodhpur, and Bozan were all in new clothes as well, and all wore turbans on their heads with red stones set in the centers. Even Kazeem had a rich new tunic, and Ishtar was sure he had polished his sword. Twelve servants gathered, carrying rolls of silk and many other rare gifts. But not the gold, frankincense, or myrrh.

"Come now," Salamar said to the group, "the time of our appointment is near."

Suddenly Jotham appeared, out of breath. "A prophetess . . ." he said, gasping. "A prophetess has told me I will find my family in a place called Bethlehem. I must go and tell Simeon and we will leave at once!"

"You're leaving?" Ishtar said.

"I must, my friend. But God be willing, we will soon meet again."

Jotham ran off in the direction of Simeon's house and Ishtar sighed a heavy sigh. "I seem to lose friends faster than I make them," he said to Kazeem.

They entered Jerusalem through what was called the Sheep Gate. It was right next to the Roman fortress of Antonio, and it made Ishtar nervous to be so close to the many Roman soldiers standing guard in red and gold uniforms, holding spears and shields.

"Halt!" The command was in Latin and sounded like it came from the general of some great army, Ishtar decided. He saw he was exactly right. Marching toward them in red robes and armor was a Roman so large he could be a tree. His face was mean, and looked like a rat. A centurion, Ishtar guessed.

"State your business in Jerusalem!" the officer ordered.

"We have an appointment with King Herod," Salamar answered.

The guard began to argue with Salamar, saying something about Jews dressed up in costumes are still Jews, but Ishtar stopped listening. Instead, he was watching a young Jewish girl about his age. She was kneeling on the stone steps that led high up to the tall bronze doors of the fortress, and she was caring for an injured Roman soldier. What he noticed most was that she had ripped a sleeve from her tunic to use as a bandage.

Before he could think another thought, Ishtar saw one of the other soldiers raise his spear and aim it at the girl. Ishtar began to form the thought that he should do something when an old man nearby knocked the spear out of the soldier's hand. There was a lot of commotion, but everything stopped when a tall Roman in a cape of red and gold, standing with his hands on his hips on a step higher than the others, yelled, "Hold!"

There was much talk between them all, during which the first soldier lowered his lance and others let go of the old man and got back in formation. Finally the tall Roman stood back from where he'd been talking to the girl. He saw her run down the steps and grab the hand of the old man, and heard the old man yell, "Tabitha! Where are we going?" He couldn't hear the reply but saw them run toward the Sheep Gate.

"A Persian?" yelled the Roman talking to Salamar. A funny look swept across the soldier's face, and Ishtar couldn't decide if it was disgust or fear. "I want no trouble with Persians!" he said.

"Then we will be on our way," Salamar said.

Ishtar smiled. Ever since Mark Antony was humiliated by the Persians in battle, the Romans had made an extra effort to avoid conflicts with Persian warriors.

Salamar and the rest headed up the street toward Herod's palace again, but Ishtar's thoughts were on the girl. Not only did she look like someone who could be his friend, she had shown no fear even against a Roman five times her size. How could such a young girl have such bravery in the face of such a powerful enemy, he wondered.

People all through the city stopped and stared as the small procession wound its way from the lower city to the upper city where rich people and rulers lived. It was much cleaner and less crowded up here, Ishtar saw, and the streets were more like those in Amaranth.

Suddenly they found themselves in a large courtyard surrounded on three sides by covered walkways, and filled in the center with gardens and trees. They crossed through the cool of the gardens to the other side where a tall archway led through a wall and into Herod's compound.

Now this is more like it, Ishtar thought. They entered another garden, one with pools and canals and waterfalls amidst palm trees, grassy terraces, and all kinds of plants. There were statues of bronze and flocks of tamed doves. Marble columns held up the roof of a covered walkway that extended around the rectangular garden. At either end, on the short sides of the rectangle, identical palaces soared into the air.

Most impressive, though, were the three towers Ishtar saw to his right. They formed a sort of triangle, and each was different, though they all were built of huge blocks of marble with differing levels of columns and terraces. So perfectly were they built that Ishtar could hardly tell where one block of marble stopped and another started.

"Prepare your mind," Salamar whispered to Ishtar. "Jewish priests and officials speak in Hebrew only." In the last hour, Ishtar realized, he'd had to speak in Aramaic, Latin, and now Hebrew. *This is just like home!* he thought.

A servant in robes of golden cloth met them and led them toward the three towers, then through more tall columns into the palace at the right end of the gardens. It all felt very familiar to Ishtar, and he thought sadly about how long he'd been gone from home. They passed pools and hallways and side rooms full of trees and flowers, then entered what Ishtar instantly identified as the throne room.

And there, upon a marble throne, sat a man that Ishtar thought surely must be as mad as a thirsty camel, and who looked just as mangy.

Why do the Romans hate the Persians so much? Why do the Persians hate the Romans? Why are Salamar and his brothers treated so poorly by the centurion?

We humans like to judge others who aren't like us so we can feel superior. We think that because we were born in a certain place, belong to a certain religion, or have certain physical features that somehow we're special. Better.

Maybe we should keep this in mind: unless we're Jewish, and were born and raised in Palestine, we're very different from Jesus in most every way.

Would we want *him* to judge *us* on that basis?

The truth is that we all have the same ancestors and come from the same family. If nothing else, as far back as Noah. So unless we're ready to disown him, there are three truths we should probably accept: we are all God's children, God loves every one of us exactly the same, and Jesus died for the person I hate just as much as he died for me.

Special Instructions for Week Four

Because Advent always starts on Sunday but Christmas is on a different day each year, Advent can last anywhere from twenty-one to twenty-eight days. Therefore the last week of *Ishtar's Odyssey* is in seven parts. The following table will help you determine which parts to read each day this week, depending on which day Christmas *Eve* falls. (See the chart on page 176.)

If Christmas Eve is on Sunday or Monday, the reading will be quite long and you may want to break it up by singing a carol or sharing in some other activity between parts.

Instead of devotional thoughts, each part is followed by a question to consider. Use the question or questions of the day as a discussion starter, or consider them seriously in your own heart. But either way, have a wonderful week: Christmas is coming!

If Christmas Eve is on:

Read these parts on:	Sun	Mon	Tues	Wed	Thur	Fri	Sat
Sunday	1–7	1–5	1–3	1–2	1–2	1	1
Monday		6–7	4–5	3–4	3	2	2
Tuesday			6–7	5	4	3	3
Wednesday				6–7	5	4	4
Thursday					6–7	5	5
Friday						6–7	6
Saturday							7

Ishtar's Odyssey

Light the violet candles and the pink candle each day.

Part One

King Herod. Ishtar thought he didn't look much like a king. His face was grey, his eyes sunken. The hair under his gold crown was long and stringy, and surely hadn't been washed in weeks. He wore fine clothes and jewels, but they hung on his body like rags on a wash line. And instead of sitting up straight and true on his throne like Sheik Konarak did, he sort of slumped across it, his legs hanging over one arm of the throne. He was reading a parchment and didn't see the visitors enter.

A servant went to Herod and whispered in his ear. The king looked up and said in a loud and rude voice, "I don't want to see anyone! Send them away." Herod spoke in Hebrew, and Ishtar wondered if he thought none of them would understand.

The servant whispered again, then Herod said, "I invited them?" Once more the servant whispered, then Herod sat straight up, threw the parchment at the servant, and said, "Ah, my good friends! Come forward and present yourselves."

Salamar, his brothers, and Ishtar all stepped forward and Salamar gave the proper introductions and greetings.

"And you are searching for this supposed . . . I mean the new king that is to be born to our people?"

"Most assuredly," Salamar said. "We saw his sign in the heavens, and have traveled many months to honor him."

Herod thought for a moment. "Then what is it you need from me?"

"We have followed a star for those many months, as I said," Salamar answered, "but now it has left us. That's when you requested we come and report to you, oh wise and noble king."

Herod stroked his beard and stared at the Persian. After several moments he stopped stroking and just stared. "My priests and prophets are incompetent. They cannot tell me exactly when this king is to be born. When did you say you saw this sign in the heavens?"

Salamar gave the exact date and time that Ishtar had first seen the star.

"These fools," Herod said, pointing at his advisors, "tell me the babe is to be born in Bethlehem, but I do not know if I can trust them."

Salamar remained silent.

"Perhaps the star will yet guide you," Herod said so softly that Ishtar could barely make out the words. His voice sounded like a sick pig now, and he sank back into the throne. "And perhaps," Herod added, "you will search Bethlehem and inform me when you find the child. I am most anxious to worship this new king with you."

Salamar bowed low. "It will be my honor to bring you any information I discover."

Herod stared again, then jumped out of his throne and screamed at the servant. "What do you mean putting goats in my bed!"

"Your . . . your majesty," the servant stammered, "I have put no . . ."

"Of course you haven't!" Herod screamed. Then deathly quiet again he added, "Don't be a fool. But make sure my breakfast is in my crown by midday tomorrow."

Then without a word to his visitors, Herod walked out of the throne room as if he were in a royal processional.

Back out in the streets a few minutes later, with the three towers of Herod's palace receding in the background, Ishtar broke the silence by saying, "Well *that* was ridiculous!"

"Yes," Salamar answered, "it certainly was."

A moment later, Ishtar noticed several squads of Herod's palace guards riding out of the horse stables, each squad headed in a different direction.

After dinner, with about an hour remaining before sunset, Kazeem was giving Ishtar his archery lesson when they both heard loud talking coming from Salamar's tent. Ishtar ran over to investigate.

Sunlight shining through the thin cloth of Salamar's tent made the inside glow from all directions, and it took Ishtar's eyes a moment to adjust. When they did, he saw the shape of a man and a boy talking to his father.

"Ishtar!" the boy-shape called out. "It is I, Bartholomew of Taricheae!"

To Think About: Why do you think Herod behaved as he did?

Part Two

Now Ishtar could see that it was indeed his fish-selling friend and there was a great reunion. Ishtar introduced Bartholomew to Kazeem, after which Bartholomew said to Salamar, "I have seen the strange star you search for! Did you find it yourself?"

Salamar nodded. "Yes. Jotham showed it to us two nights ago, and it led us in the direction of Jerusalem."

"We met your king, Herod," Ishtar said excitedly. "He was most anxious to worship your messiah when he is born. Father promised to tell him when we find the child."

Nathan, who had been standing back, finally spoke up. "I came to rescue two boys lost in the desert but I seem to be the only one who doesn't know what's going on!" Salamar laughed, and sat his friend down to catch him up on the news. Bartholomew told Ishtar and Salamar an amazing story of being attacked by Romans the same day he traded with Salamar for some Persian tea. His family had been taken captive and was still missing. Ishtar couldn't believe that another of his new friends had lived through such adventures.

"We saw those Romans!" Ishtar gasped. Then he told how they had seen the legion of soldiers marching across the hills after the caravan left Taricheae.

When Bartholomew heard that Jotham had left for a town called Bethlehem earlier in the day, he was anxious to go there. But Nathan said it was too late, and it would have to wait until morning. Salamar asked Bartholomew about his family, and while Bartholomew told him, Nathan invited Ishtar to walk with him.

It was dusk by now, and the people of the caravan were settling in around their fires. Ishtar kept looking at Nathan out of the corner of his eye. Finally he said, "Why is it that everyone calls you a fool? You look very normal to me."

Nathan laughed loudly. "Do not let appearances trick you, my young friend. I am indeed foolish." Ishtar had no idea what the man was saying, so Nathan added, "At times I dress and play the part of a fool. I find it better to fight with trickery than with the sword."

They turned and walked down the hill toward the stream Kidron, Kazeem following a short distance behind.

"So, Ishtar, have you yet found your role in this drama?" Nathan asked.

"What do you mean, my role?"

"It seems that Jehovah is bringing many things together for a most holy event. Jotham is here for a reason, Bartholomew is here for a reason, your father and I are both here for a reason. Have you yet discovered your own purpose?"

Ishtar shrugged. "I am only here because my father made me come."

By now they had reached the stream. Ishtar sat on a rock and soaked his feet, Nathan sat on another stone next to him.

"I do not believe that to be true, Ishtar," Nathan said. "If you are here, it is because Jehovah wants you here."

"Jehovah is one of your gods, correct?" Ishtar asked.

Nathan smiled. "Jehovah is my *only* God. Jehovah is the only God there is."

Ishtar desperately wanted to tell this old fool that such thoughts were ridiculous, but remembering how that had gotten him into trouble in the past, he held his tongue. Instead he said, "Why do you believe there is only one god when it makes no sense?"

Nathan took a deep breath. "Indeed, it is the only thing that *does* make sense. How can there be more than one in charge of a thing? Is not a fine meal prepared by many, but all led by one cook? Does not a group of musicians have but one player providing the beat of the music? Is not this mighty caravan of yours led by one *karvan-salar*? There is only one God because there can *be* only one God."

"But why do you think *your* god is the only *real* god?"

Nathan was quiet for a moment, then said, "Because he has told me so. He has told me through my ancestor Noah. He has told me through my ancestor Abraham. He has told me through my ancestors Moses, and Elijah, and David, through the prophets and the judges, the stories of whom are all written in our Torah." Nathan stood and waded into the stream to wash his feet. "But if that were all the evidence I had my faith would be dead. You see," he said as he turned and looked at Ishtar, "he has also spoken to my heart, and is always near. And sometime soon, he will speak to me through the Messiah."

"I know many languages," Ishtar said, "and Simeon tried to explain, but I still do not understand this word, *messiah*."

"Ahh, it is a most wonderful word," Nathan answered. "It means 'one who will save us.'"

Now Ishtar stood and waded across the stream, enjoying the feel of smooth rocks on the soles of his feet but feeling frustrated inside. "Save us from *what*? Our Jewish *karvan-salar* said this messiah will save us from the Romans. But I'm already saved from them."

Nathan thought for a moment. "No, not the Romans. Save us from ourselves, really. Save us from our selfish desires, from our need to feel important and to be the center of attention, when it is God himself on whom we should be centered. Like the water of this stream washing our feet," Nathan said, "the love of the Messiah will wash our souls of selfishness. If we allow him to."

Ishtar scrunched up his face. "That's what Simeon said. But how can one man's love wash the souls of everyone else?"

Nathan smiled. "Because the Messiah is not just a man. *He is God himself!*" And then Nathan told Ishtar a most amazing story, a story of laws, and prophets. A story of love, and of sacrifice. A story such as Ishtar had never heard in all his lessons, or in all his life.

To Think About: How has God prepared Ishtar throughout the journey to hear the story Nathan tells?

Part Three

Later that evening, after a fine meal of celebration, Ishtar and Bartholomew lay talking on their sleeping mats outside Ishtar's tent.

"Our *karvan-salar* said that Jews live under laws meant to keep their feet on safe paths," Ishtar said, "so why do you need a messiah?"

"Well," Bartholomew said, "Nathan says the Messiah will somehow change all that. We have lived under God's laws for many centuries, but we always end up doing something wrong and getting into trouble with him."

"What do you think this new messiah will be like?" Ishtar asked.

It was silent a long time before Bartholomew answered. "I think he will be much like Nathan," he said finally. "Nathan will give up anything to help anyone, and never ask anything for himself. And I think that's what the Messiah will be like."

They talked for a long time about Jotham, and Nathan, and the Messiah. Ishtar told Bartholomew about the girl he'd seen stand up to the Romans and Bartholomew said, "That sounds like my friend Tabitha," and Ishtar said yes, that was the name the old man called her. They were just about ready to sleep when a bright light from the center of the camp lit up the sky.

"What is *that*?" Ishtar yelled, sitting up.

"I do not *know!*" Bartholomew answered. "Perhaps a tent is on fire!"

The boys looked around, but no one else seemed to have noticed, or they were all asleep, because nothing moved anywhere in the camp. Bartholomew stood and tugged at Ishtar's tunic. "Come on!"

Ishtar pulled away. "We cannot!" he said. "I am forbidden to leave my tent once my father puts me to bed."

Bartholomew looked at Ishtar with disgust. "We *must* go look at this thing!" he said. "Your father would surely understand!"

Ishtar looked at Mahmoud, who was his bodyguard on duty. Mahmoud was much more lenient than Kazeem, and usually let Ishtar do what he wanted. Then he looked at Bartholomew and shook his head. "You are just like Jotham!" he said. "You're going to get us in trouble." But he got up out of his bed and followed Bartholomew through the little village of tents.

Just past the tents of his uncle Jodhpur's wives, Ishtar saw the source of the light: Salamar's tent. It glowed like a bonfire—just like it had in the sunshine earlier, but now it was as if the sun was *inside* the tent. It puffed outward as if some great wind were blowing, but the air was still. The tent seemed to be on fire, but it did not burn. Slowly the boys moved forward, wanting neither to be caught out of bed nor to interrupt some feast that was only for adults. But the light was so brilliant and the air so full of a sweet scent like honeysuckle that Ishtar could not hold himself back.

Ishtar stepped toward his father's tent. He reached out as carefully as if he were reaching for a scorpion and took the edge of the tent flap between two fingers. When he pulled it back, what they saw made both boys gasp. Salamar was turned away from them, lying face down flat on the floor. On the other side of him was an angel, its wings moving slowly, shining as brightly as the sun, and speaking words that filled the air with fragrance.

The light radiating from the angel shimmered like the waves of heat above a fire. It was like looking at all the gold and diamonds in Sheik Konarak's throne room, Ishtar thought. The brightness of the light did not hurt Ishtar's eyes, but somehow the sight was so . . . so holy that he could not bear to look at it. He covered his face with his fingers and fell to the ground as the angel spoke.

"And so Jehovah has sent me with this message for you, Salamar of Persia," the angel said. "Do not trust the king called Herod, for he is not the true King of the Jews. Follow the star, and when you have found the babe, worship him in secret. For the forces of Herod are cruel and mighty. But the kingdom of God awaits him who obeys. Glory to God in the highest!" the angel boomed out, and the sound rattled the ground. "And on earth, peace, for this is the night of the Messiah's birth!"

Suddenly the tent was dark again. Slowly, Ishtar raised his head, as did Bartholomew and Salamar. The angel was gone, and Ishtar examined his arms and legs, expecting them to be burned as if from the sun. Neither boy could speak. They just looked dumbly from each other to the front of the tent where the angel had stood, and back again. Salamar, too, sat in shock, until he slowly turned around at the sound of the boys' shuffling.

"Ishtar," he wheezed. "Did you see this thing? Did you hear?"

"Yes, Father," Ishtar answered weakly.

"Then go and wake my brothers. Tell them we must leave at once!"

To Think About: How do you think you'd respond if God sent an angel to talk to *you*?

Part Four

Soon the whole camp was awake and chattering as Nathan, Salamar, and Ishtar's two uncles consulted. Finally Salamar turned and addressed the whole camp.

"We have decided that the caravan shall remain here," he said loudly enough to be heard, but not so loud his voice would carry beyond the edges of their camp. "If the entire caravan leaves, Herod will be alerted and send spies. My brothers and I and a few dozen men will follow the star when it appears," he said. "We shall take only a few tents and enough food for a day. Nathan, my son, and the boy Bartholomew will accompany us."

Bartholomew and Ishtar looked at each other and grinned.

"I believe I know where the star will lead you, my friend," Nathan said to Salamar. "If you like, we could start in that direction."

Salamar thought for a moment. "No, we will wait for the star. Perhaps you do know where this messiah will be born. But we must find him in our own way."

Nathan smiled and nodded, understanding. Suddenly someone shouted, and everyone looked to the sky. "The star!" Ishtar gasped.

Quickly a few tents were taken down and packed onto camels, along with other provisions. Then the small band started out, following the star up the Kidron Valley and toward the south.

"Jotham said that the messiah is coming for all people, not just you Jews," Ishtar said as he walked beside Bartholomew.

"It is as Nathan has told us," Bartholomew answered.

Ishtar looked at Nathan, who walked ahead of them. Nathan was rubbing his stomach as if in pain. "I believe I would like having only one god," he said as he watched Nathan. "Perhaps he would answer more prayers than our other gods do."

As all the excitement of seeing the angel and the hasty departure passed, Ishtar began to feel sleepy. His head kept nodding as he walked, and he felt as if a soft pillow were stuffed inside his skull. Bartholomew, too, kept stumbling beside him, and Ishtar wished he'd brought Musa along to ride.

But then the line came to a sudden stop and the boys were instantly awake again. They ran to the front of the little caravan and found Salamar and the other men staring into the sky.

"What is it, Father?" Ishtar asked.

"The star," the older man answered. "It has disappeared again."

Both boys searched the sky, but the special star was nowhere to be seen. Then someone yelled, "Look!" and all eyes turned to a little hill across a valley to their right. There, in the dark, sat a small village, covering the top of the hill like snow on a mountain.

"Bethlehem," Nathan said.

"A quiet town," Salamar commented. Then with a sigh he said, "We shall camp here, alongside the road, until the star again appears."

"I believe the star was leading you to that town," Nathan said to his friend.

"Yes!" Ishtar added. "Remember the scroll?"

Salamar just shrugged. "Perhaps. But until it guides us directly into the village, or wherever it is taking us, we shall camp here."

A short time later Kazeem had pitched Ishtar's tent. Half the men were already asleep on the ground, the other half stood guard. Ishtar looked around to find Nathan and Bartholomew and finally saw them at the edge of the road, looking down at the valley below and across it to Bethlehem. He couldn't hear their words, but it looked like Bartholomew was upset, and trying to convince Nathan of something. Finally they came back over to Salamar, so Ishtar joined them. "Salamar, my friend," Nathan said with a smile, "I believe I shall send Bartholomew into Bethlehem to fetch me some fresh dates. May I send your son with him?"

"Dates, at this time of night?" Salamar said.

"For the peace of my inner workings," Nathan said. "My body is objecting to the trek my soul has taken it on."

With a wave of his hand Salamar said, "Oh that! We have some fine potions that will ease your pain. Some crushed water lily perhaps, or roasted locusts."

Nathan shook his head. "No, no," he said, "those things are strangers to my body. I must have some fresh dates."

Salamar sighed. "Very well. My son may accompany your charge."

"Thank you, my friend," Nathan replied. Then he turned to Bartholomew and handed him some money, saying, "Be sure to hurry back if you find that which you seek!"

Ishtar had a feeling there was a double meaning to his words.

To Think About: If God is protecting Salamar and the caravan, why would they have to worry about Herod?

Part Five

Ishtar and Bartholomew ran out of the camp and across the valley toward Bethlehem with Kazeem close behind. There were many shepherds camped here, and the two boys had to weave their way around goatskin tents and corrals of sheep. Finally they climbed up the other side of the valley and onto the road just where it entered Bethlehem. As they walked into the little town they passed a man leading a donkey. On the donkey sat a young woman weeping softly. Ishtar could tell she would soon give birth.

"Good sir," Bartholomew called to the man. "May I be of service? Your wife weeps, and it is many hours until morning. Is there a need I can meet for you?"

The man stopped walking and turned back to the boys. "I fear not," he said. "My wife is in the pains of childbirth, but I can find no place for her to lay her head. I have been turned away from every inn in Bethlehem."

"Surely there is at least *one* bed in all of Bethlehem! Would you follow me so I may search for you?"

The man hesitated, then his wife let out a little cry and he said, "Yes, yes, we shall try again!"

"What are we looking for?" Ishtar asked as Bartholomew searched the town.

"I will know when I find it," the other boy answered.

Finally Bartholomew let out a yell. With Ishtar on his heels, he ran up a dirt path to the wooden door of an inn and knocked.

Just then the woman on the donkey cried out loudly. Ishtar ran back out to her on the street and saw her husband trying to help her off the donkey. Had a roaming band of thieves been running toward him the man could not have looked more terrified. The woman cried out again and Ishtar saw that her feet were far from touching the ground—about the distance of a . . .

Without thought and without asking, Ishtar sprang to the side of the donkey and dropped down on all fours. A moment later the woman's feet set down on his back. With her husband's help she carefully stepped down to the ground. Kazeem stood back in the shadows watching and for a moment Ishtar was angry that he hadn't come to help. Then he remembered his bodyguard's words back at the devil sand and understood that to help the woman would mean letting down his guard for Ishtar.

Ishtar stood and saw that Bartholomew was talking with a man at the door of the inn.

"Thank you, boy," the woman said, and Ishtar thought her voice sounded like the cooing of doves. "That was an act of great kindness, and I fear I have nothing with which to repay you."

Ishtar bowed. "No payment is asked or required," he said. "I gladly offer my services to one so sublime."

Bartholomew ran up and said his new friend Hasrah would allow the couple to sleep in his stable below the inn. "He just sent for a boy to fetch some clean hay. Can I assist you in any other way?" he asked.

"You have given us much already, and we can manage from here," the man said. "Unless you happen to know where there is a midwife?"

"My apologies," Bartholomew said, "but I am a visitor here myself, and know no one in this town."

"I understand. Have no concern for us, we shall be fine."

"Then I will leave you with these generous people," Bartholomew answered, "as I go my own way to complete my own journey." Then he and Ishtar turned the corner and set out to search for the Messiah.

"Perhaps we should look in a temple," Ishtar suggested. "That would seem a most likely place for a god to be born."

"I don't think they *have* a temple," Bartholomew said. "The town is too small."

"Well then, where *will* we look?"

"Nathan said it could be anywhere. We will just have to go from house to house listening for the crying of a newborn baby."

"There must be many babies here. How will we know which one?"

"Oh, I will know the Messiah when I hear him," Bartholomew said. "All I have to do is hear his cry and I will know. Such a holy thing cannot be hidden!"

As the boys walked up and down the streets of Bethlehem, Kazeem stepped forward and whispered in Ishtar's ear. "Perhaps the woman you helped was the woman Bartholomew seeks."

"I thought of that too," Ishtar answered, "but I wish not to suggest that my friend failed to recognize the mother of his messiah."

"But we are probably walking away from that which he seeks."

Ishtar shrugged. "It's his country. I must let him set the path of our feet."

The boys craned their necks this way and that to listen for the cries of babies. They heard one, down a little side street, and saw through a window a mother walking her baby by lamp-light. "That is not him," Bartholomew said quickly. "That is not the mother of a Messiah. I can tell such things. The moment I see her I will know she is the one," he said confidently.

For several minutes they searched, reaching finally the edge of the town where many shepherds were camped in the fields below. Bartholomew saw several standing around a fire near a tall tree, then froze in fear. "Ishtar!" he hissed. "We must leave this place!"

Ishtar started to protest but Bartholomew clamped his hand over his friend's8 mouth. "That man is Decha of Megiddo!" he whispered.

Memories of Decha chasing him through the tunnels slithered up Ishtar's spine. *Surely he will kill me if he sees me*, he thought. Then he looked to make sure Kazeem was close by.

To Think About: Bartholomew is certain he'll recognize Jesus the moment he sees the child's parents, but then doesn't. Do you think that ever happens to us? Do you think God ever sends people to show us Jesus, and we don't recognize that blessing?

Part Six

The sound of their sandals echoed off the walls as the boys ran back through the town. At one point Ishtar heard a woman scream, and realized it came from the stable where they had left the pregnant woman. Bartholomew was many paces ahead now and had just passed an intersection with another street when a young girl ran around the corner behind him. Ishtar smacked right into her and the two bounced off each other.

"Oh! I am so sorry!" Ishtar said. "May I be . . ."

But by then the girl had nodded a quick apology and continued on her way. Right behind her a woman followed, trying to keep up, and they both ran down the little ramp into the stable. It took Ishtar only a moment to realize the woman Bartholomew had helped was giving birth, and the woman who ran by him must be a midwife.

Half a second later Ishtar realized the girl was Tabitha, the same one he'd seen tending to the Roman soldier in Jerusalem. What kind of girl was this who had courage to stand up to Romans and was unafraid to run alone through city streets in the middle of the night? For a moment Ishtar wished *he* had such courage. Then he caught up with Bartholomew and the two boys raced back to the caravan.

"Nathan!" Bartholomew cried as they approached. "Nathan! Come quickly!"

Nathan was sitting across a fire from Salamar as the Persian searched the sky. "What is it?"

"Decha of Megiddo camps outside Bethlehem and surely plots evil!"

At the name of Decha, Nathan jumped up and spun around to look out across the valley toward Bethlehem. "Where!" was all he said.

Bartholomew searched the darkness for a moment, then pointed and said, "There! By that tall tree!"

Nathan looked back at Salamar. "This is a thing I must do," he said. "You must remain here and follow the path Jehovah has set for you. I will go alone to meet Decha."

Salamar nodded.

"No!" Bartholomew screamed. "We must *all* go! We must fight this thief and kill him!"

Nathan held Bartholomew firmly by the shoulders. "No, child. This is the work of a man. And a fool. The fight I must now fight is mine alone. It is why," he said, looking again at the valley, "Jehovah has brought me to this place."

Just then the faint cries of, "Father! Father!" were heard, echoing up from the valley. Everyone looked to see a small boy, about the size of Ishtar, running across the fields toward a man who was yelling, "Jotham!" Instantly Ishtar put the pieces of the puzzle together and realized his friend Jotham had finally found his father.

But a moment later a dark form swept out of the shadows and came between father and son. Two other men captured the father, and in a moment were holding him captive with ropes tied to his wrists.

"Decha!" Nathan spat. Then turning to the rest of the group he said, "I must go!"

Salamar held Bartholomew tightly as Nathan raced down the hill. Frustration clamped around Ishtar's chest like a bony hand. He wanted to help Bartholomew, wanted to help Nathan, but felt completely useless. To his horror, he saw Decha take a huge swing of his sword, aiming right for the neck of Jotham's father.

Just then Nathan came cartwheeling out of the woods and landed between Decha and his target. Ishtar could not hear what was happening, but watched as Nathan flipped and slid and twirled around in a great fool's act. Finally he landed right in front of Decha, plucked the sword from the thief's hands, and spun away to safety.

"There!" Bartholomew cried, tugging at Salamar's arms. "Nathan has won. Now may I please go to my friend Jotham?"

Salamar hesitated, but then said, "Very well. It seems Nathan has indeed taken control." Ishtar watched for a moment as Bartholomew ran down the hill, but then something in the sky caught his attention. An ancient olive tree blocked his view, so he moved over into the road until he could see. "The star!" he gasped softly. There it was, as it had been for so many months, hanging in the sky at the crown of *Sagr*. But something was different this time . . . something was strange.

"Father!" Ishtar called, not taking his eyes off the sky. "The star!"

But Salamar paid no attention—he was too busy watching the events in the valley below.

Ishtar now saw something he'd never seen in the sky in all his life: the star was getting bigger. As he watched, he could tell that the star was moving toward him.

After another moment Ishtar broke his gaze and ran over to Salamar. "Father! Father! The star . . ."

Ishtar stopped short when he saw an amazing sight in the valley as well: Jotham was rejoicing with his family. Salamar explained that Decha and all his men were dead or chased away because of Bartholomew and Nathan, who were just coming up the hill. A moment later Salamar greeted his old friend warmly. He called for a great feast of celebration, and was giving orders to have it prepared, when suddenly the whole valley was filled with a brilliant light, brighter than the sun.

"The star!" Ishtar cried out. But then he saw it was no star at all, but an angel, and the same angel he had seen in Salamar's tent earlier.

In the valley below, people screamed and men drew their swords. Here on the hill, Bartholomew, Nathan, Salamar, and all their men fell on their faces and covered their heads. But Ishtar stood and stared, completely unafraid. The light spread out until it seemed to cover the entire sky, then a voice, loud and deep, came booming from above.

"Do not be afraid," the voice said, "for behold, I bring you good tidings of great joy, that will be for all the people." He hovered in the air, light shining from his very being. He held a trumpet in his right hand and a golden scepter in his left.

"Today in the town of David," the angel continued, "a savior has been born to you; he is Christ the Lord. This will be a sign to you: You will find a baby wrapped in cloths and lying in a manger."

Suddenly from nowhere there appeared thousands of angels, some near, some far. They covered the sky for as far as Ishtar could see, and lit up the world with their glow.

As they appeared, the angels began to sing. "Glory to God," they sang, and it was the most beautiful sound Ishtar had ever heard. "Glory to God in the highest, and on earth peace to men on whom his favor rests!"

Over and over the angels sang, "Glory to God in the highest."

And then, quite suddenly, it was quiet.

Slowly, the others stood to their feet. "The Messiah has been born," Nathan whispered.

Bartholomew whipped around and looked Nathan square in the eye. "I'm as dumb as a donkey!" he cried.

"Bartholomew!" Nathan said. "What is it?"

"The woman! The pregnant woman! I was right there next to her . . ." Then he pulled on Nathan's arm. "Come on!" He turned and started down the hill.

"Slow down, boy! You'll run straight out of your tunic!" Nathan yelled.

Below them, Ishtar could see that Jotham, too, was running toward Bethlehem, with his entire clan following him. And on the far side of the valley he saw the girl Tabitha. She, too, was leading her family in the direction of the stable.

But a moment later Ishtar saw something that threatened to destroy all of them and the baby messiah too.

To Think About: Why was everyone afraid when the angel appeared?

Part Seven

Far to the left of Bethlehem some movement in the hills had caught Ishtar's eye. He stared through the dark for a long moment, trying to discern shadow from shadow. Then he remembered how Jotham had taught him to look just to the side of a thing you want to see in the dark.

Suddenly he understood what he was seeing: men on horses. Moments later he could see they carried the long spears and wore the uniforms of King Herod's soldiers.

"Father! Look!" he cried.

Salamar looked where Ishtar pointed but saw nothing.

"It's a squad of soldiers from Herod!"

Salamar sighed heavily, but made no move.

"You must send your men to scare them off or they will harm our friends and find the messiah!" Ishtar pleaded.

"Ishtar, I should think you'd understand by now that we do not follow the whims of men, the orders of foreign kings, or the folly of our own hearts. We follow only the stars."

"They'll kill them all!" Ishtar shouted. "How can you stand there and do *nothing!*"

Salamar dropped to one knee and looked Ishtar straight in the eye. "I am not doing nothing," he said gently. "I am doing my duty, and obeying the commands of my sheik. I have sworn my life to him, and I yield to the higher authority of the heavens. Right now, they all demand that I stay right where I am."

Ishtar started to protest again but Salamar stopped him with one finger on the boy's lips. "But there is one," Salamar continued, "who is bound by no such oath. There is one in this camp tonight who is free to lead men into battle, to save Jotham, and Bartholomew, and the newborn king."

Ishtar scanned the faces of the camp. Not his uncles, he decided—they were bound by the same oath as his father. Surely not the servants, not even Kazeem, who was a brave man but could not legally give orders to others. Ishtar looked back at his father with furrowed brow. "Who?" he asked

Salamar leaned in even closer and whispered in Ishtar's ear. "It is you," he said, "son of a counselor to the Sheik of Amaranth, a prince of Persia by right and tradition. A man of honor, of wit, and courage. You must lead the rescue," Salamar concluded, "or I fear for the lives of our friends."

"That's ridiculous!" Ishtar yelled. He broke away from his father, paced wildly around the fire, a thousand wasps buzzing in his head. He wished he were back in Amaranth with his servants and baths and fine linens. He wished he had never been forced to come on this stupid trip, to spend his days covered in dust, sore and exhausted. How could he, a mere boy, lead a rescue? Was he not full of fear? His father had lied! *There is no honor inside me*, Ishtar thought. *No wit! And certainly no courage!*

But then Ishtar's thoughts turned to the many events of the last several months. In that time he had turned eleven—still a boy, but on the precipice of manhood. In those months he had learned to endure hard days without a second thought, had learned to take in stride discomfort, and hunger, and scorching hot desert. He had talked to many people, had encountered many ideas, had learned many things.

And then he remembered the story Nathan had told him, a story about the god Jehovah, and Ishtar's role in Jehovah's plans . . .

At that moment a new thought struck Ishtar and he stopped dead in his tracks. He looked again at Jotham and Bartholomew, almost to Bethlehem's edge now. He watched Tabitha, and thought of the courage she showed in facing down the Romans. He turned slightly and saw Herod's men closing in on the town. Perhaps, Ishtar thought to himself, perhaps there now resides inside me something else. Perhaps just a bit of . . .

Suddenly Ishtar turned back to the camp. He saw the eyes of his father watching him, as well as the eyes of his uncles, and Kazeem, and all the other men. Without another word to his father he yelled, "Kazeem! Gather ten of our best men, and bring me my horse. Prepare for battle!"

Ishtar was amazed that the camp immediately sprang into action on his orders. He leaped onto his horse as the other men and Kazeem rode up on theirs. "If there be a god of the Jews," he yelled, "may he ride with us tonight!"

With another yell Ishtar led the band of twelve down the road at breakneck speed. As Kazeem had taught him on the journey across the desert, he trusted his horse to see and follow the road while he himself kept an eye on Herod's thugs. *There's only one more corner in the road*, he realized, *before those thugs will be able to see all the commotion in Bethlehem and know something has happened*. He whipped his horse to run faster.

Ishtar reached the curve in the road just before Herod's men would round it. He yelled over his shoulder, "Six to the left, six to the right! Show them the Parthian shot!" In a moment Ishtar and his men surrounded the soldiers in two circles moving opposite directions. Every one of them shot their arrows backwards from their mounts. The arrows stabbed the ground in front of Herod's men who were completely confused and terrified.

Ishtar gave a yell and the Persians slid to a stop, dirt and rock flying, with Ishtar in the middle of the road directly in front of the leader. A moment earlier Herod's men had been sleepy with routine, but now snapped alert and reached for their weapons.

"Hold!" Ishtar yelled, and suddenly there was silence.

The leader finally found his voice and growled, "Who is it that commands a squadron of the mighty King Herod to hold?"

"It is I, Ishtar," he yelled, standing tall in his stirrups, "Prince of Persia, son of Salamar, Royal Advisor to his highness Sheik Konarak, commander of the Parthian armies, ruler of half the peoples of the known world, decider of the fate of millions . . ." Ishtar stopped, sat back in his saddle, leaned forward toward the leader, looked him straight in the eye and whispered, "or of one."

The leader found his wits again and said, "Move aside. We have been sent by King Herod himself to search the town of Bethlehem. Why should I fear a sheik who sends a small boy to do his bidding?"

Ishtar kicked his horse softly and walked it forward until his face was inches from the other leader. "I have stared the cobra in the face and won the contest," he said, speaking in Hebrew now. "I have felt the grasp of devil sand around my knees and walked away from its death. I have had my animal shot out from under me, had my enemies attempt to poison me, and outsmarted the sting of the scorpion. I have captured an assassin through wit and cunning, and have led my people across the desert Badiyat Ash Sham in the face of a shamal sandstorm. I have overcome all this and more, and survived it either on my own strength or with the protection of the gods. Either way, I suggest you take me seriously."

The leader gulped, looked around nervously at the men and horses that surrounded them, then back at Ishtar. "What it is I can do for Ishtar, Prince of Persia?"

As if conspiring with a fellow thief, Ishtar said, "You can turn around and leave this place at once. This is *my* territory. I am here doing that which Herod requests, and Herod has charged me with reporting to him the location of the new Jewish king. I myself searched Bethlehem not two hours ago and tell you truthfully that I have seen no child king there. Now go your way, and search where no one has yet searched. It is an insult to me, to my sheik, and to all of Persia to presume you need to supervise us."

The leader took another long moment to think. He looked again at the Persian warriors surrounding him, then without another word to Ishtar gave the order for his men to go back the way they had come.

Ishtar's men relaxed, gave a shout of victory, and congratulated him on his courage and guile.

Kazeem just sat back in his saddle and smiled.

As they rode back toward the rest of their group Ishtar looked toward the heavens and said under his breath, "Finally! A God who answers prayers!"

Halfway back to the campsite they met up with Salamar and the others headed up the road toward them. "The soldiers of Herod have decided they should go home for the night," Ishtar reported to his father.

"And we are headed toward Bethlehem," his father reported to Ishtar. "The star has told us it is time to visit this new king!"

To Think About: What are the many ways God watched over Ishtar throughout the story, and led him to the place where God could use him to do good?

CHRISTMAS MORNING

Messiah

Light all the candles.

Salamar, Bozan, and Jodhpur had all changed into their finest clothes, with turbans atop their heads. Ishtar quickly threw on the formal tunic Salamar had brought for him. At the edge of Bethlehem, the small party tied their horses to posts, and Ishtar led them on foot through the twists and turns of the narrow streets.

Soon they arrived at the inn of Hasrah and saw that the streets and the ramp down to the stable were full of shepherds buzzing about the events of the evening. When the shepherds saw the three magi marching toward them, they stopped talking and opened a path down to the stable.

Several lamps had been lit and hung around the stable. As Ishtar entered he could see that it was full of people. In the center of it all was a tiny baby, wrapped in swaddling clothes, and lying in a manger.

At once Ishtar's heart swelled with love for the child. He could never—not that night or any other—exactly say what it was that filled him with such adoration for the baby. But what he felt was real, and what he knew was that this, indeed, was the son of a god.

Salamar, Jodhpur, and Bozan stepped forward, dropped to their knees, and bowed before the babe. They held out the gifts they'd been carrying for so many months and so many miles—a treasure chest of gold, an urn of frankincense, and boxes of myrrh.

"We bring you greetings and tribute from his highness Sheik Konarak of Amaranth," Salamar said softly to the child, "and his prayer that your wisdom and compassion may shine on all people, now and for all generations to come."

The man and woman Ishtar had helped earlier were sitting next to the manger and now thanked the magi for the generous gifts.

Salamar and his brothers rose, and that's when introductions began. First Ishtar introduced his father to Mary and Joseph, then Jotham introduced *his* parents to Ishtar and Salamar. There were introductions from Bartholomew and his whole family, and Tabitha and hers, and of course Nathan the sometimes fool was in the middle of the whole thing.

For some time they all celebrated together, and speculated on the wondrous things this child-king would do. Then Salamar turned to his son and said quietly, "Ishtar, it is time for us to leave, before we burden our hosts beyond their hospitality."

Ishtar was sad, but Salamar assured him they'd visit again the next day, before heading back to Amaranth. So they said their goodbyes, then mounted their horses and followed the road back up the hill. Salamar surprised Ishtar with a package of baklava, zulbia, and gaz which was passed around to all the men.

"So tell me, my son," Salamar said as Ishtar rode alongside him. "What have you learned on this long journey?"

"I have learned there are not as many ridiculous things in the world as I thought," Ishtar answered. "There are just things I do not yet know."

"And what are some of those ridiculous things you now believe to be true?"

Ishtar thought for a moment, until the truthful answer appeared inside his brain. He was afraid of that answer, afraid of what his father would think, afraid his father would be angry with him. But then he looked back down the hill, where he could see over the rooftops the little stable still glowing in the night, still surrounded by people. He saw through the doorway and over the tops of the heads of the worshipers to the rough little manger. And he saw the tiny baby swaddled inside. Then he threw back his shoulders, turned to his father, and said, "I believe, Father, that the baby Jesus is the Messiah of all people, the King of all Kings, the son of the one true God!"

For unto *you* is born a Savior, Christ the Lord, who came to earth to tell you, and show you, and help you believe, the great and selfless love God has for you, and that you can have for others.

Advent Through the Years

The following chart gives the Sunday on which Advent begins and the day of the week on which Christmas Eve falls, for the next several decades:

Year	Advent begins	Christmas Eve is	Year	Advent begins	Christmas Eve is	Year	Advent begins	Christmas Eve is
2010	November 28	Friday	2034	December 3	Sunday	2058	December 1	Tuesday
2011	November 27	Saturday	2035	December 2	Monday	2059	November 30	Wednesday
2012	December 2	Monday	2036	November 30	Wednesday	2060	November 28	Friday
2013	December 1	Tuesday	2037	November 29	Thursday	2061	November 27	Saturday
2014	November 30	Wednesday	2038	November 28	Friday	2062	December 3	Sunday
2015	November 29	Thursday	2039	November 27	Saturday	2063	December 2	Monday
2016	November 27	Saturday	2040	December 2	Monday	2064	November 30	Wednesday
2017	December 3	Sunday	2041	December 1	Tuesday	2065	November 29	Thursday
2018	December 2	Monday	2042	November 30	Wednesday	2066	November 28	Friday
2019	December 1	Tuesday	2043	November 29	Thursday	2067	November 27	Saturday
2020	November 29	Thursday	2044	November 27	Saturday	2068	December 2	Monday
2021	November 28	Friday	2045	December 3	Sunday	2069	December 1	Tuesday
2022	November 27	Saturday	2046	December 2	Monday	2070	November 30	Wednesday
2023	December 3	Sunday	2047	December 1	Tuesday	2071	November 29	Thursday
2024	December 1	Tuesday	2048	November 29	Thursday	2072	November 27	Saturday
2025	November 30	Wednesday	2049	November 28	Friday	2073	December 3	Sunday
2026	November 29	Thursday	2050	November 27	Saturday	2074	December 2	Monday
2027	November 28	Friday	2051	December 3	Sunday	2075	December 1	Tuesday
2028	December 3	Sunday	2052	December 1	Tuesday	2076	November 29	Thursday
2029	December 2	Monday	2053	November 30	Wednesday	2077	November 28	Friday
2030	December 1	Tuesday	2054	November 29	Thursday	2078	November 27	Saturday
2031	November 30	Wednesday	2055	November 28	Friday	2079	December 3	Sunday
2032	November 28	Friday	2056	December 3	Sunday	2080	December 1	Tuesday
2033	November 27	Saturday	2057	December 2	Monday	2081	November 30	Wednesday